Rebecca's Reveries

by Marnie L. Pehrson

First Edition 2004

Published by CES BUSINESS CONSULTANTS
Copyright 2004 Marnie L. Pehrson
Cover photos by Marnie L. Pehrson
All Rights Reserved.

*All characters within this story are fictional.
Any resemblance to real people living or
dead is purely coincidental.*

Printed in the United States of America

ISBN: 0-9729750-2-0

To Laurel,

*for the laughs, the tears and years
ahead when you'll look back and realize
your mother wasn't as crazy as
you thought she was.*

Special Thanks to Amy

*for the brainstorming sessions,
constant encouragement and hysterical instant
messages. Couldn't have done it without you!*

Chapter 1

Rebecca Marchant slumped in the window seat of her bedroom, leaning her shoulder against the dormer window pane. While her dark brown eyes gazed intently on the bright summer day, she remained completely oblivious to the birds chirping outside her window, the crystal clear blue skies and the roses blooming in her mother's flower garden. A solitary tear streamed down her cheek and landed on her hands which were folded in front of her, resting on the window sill.

The days leading up to and including her mother's funeral were busy, people bustling about helping, bringing a plethora of food and condolences. The lonely weeks following were quiet. Her once jovial father remained sequestered in his study brooding, working constantly and mourning the loss of his life's love. He ate little, and slept even less. What sleep he did obtain was not in his bedroom, but on a couch in his study. Months had passed since her mother's death and the tear trailing down Rebecca's cheek at that moment was not for the loss of her mother, whom she loved and missed, but for the absence of her father's companionship.

Gone were the evenings they spent together riding horseback. Gone were the horse races and competitions, the

4

steeplechases and cheering for the family's entry in the qualifying races of the Kentucky Derby. The Kentucky Derby would be held within the next few days and Rebecca lamented that it would be the first one she and her father had missed for as long as she could remember.

Rebecca, shook from her reverie by a horse drawn carriage pulling up into the circular driveway, rose to her feet and crossed to her mirror, brushing the tears from her eyes and straightening her sleek dark black hair. She hated to appear teary-eyed in front of her Aunt Miriam so she dabbed at the corner of her eyes with her handkerchief, pinched her high cheekbones, widened her deep brown eyes, and pasted on a smile in an effort to appear cheerful. Aunt Miriam wouldn't stand for "pity-wallowin'" as she put it. She loved her younger sister, Caroline, in a way no one else could, but she had had her fill of Ethan Marchant's constant brooding and inability to continue with his life. She worried for his health and grew more concerned with each passing day that sixteen-year-old Rebecca's youth wasted away. Miriam made two or three visits each week to the house to check on Rebecca, seeing that she was well cared for and attempting to fill the void caused by Caroline's passing.

Rebecca wore her cheerful smile down the steps and opened the door for her aunt, "Aunt Miriam! So wonderful to see you!" Rebecca threw her arms around her Aunt who returned her embrace. Miriam had a youthful glow about her. In her early forties, she had managed to escape the onset of wrinkles. She swept her beautiful blonde hair atop her head and wore a bright blue hat that matched her exceptional blue eyes. Miriam loved bright colors that matched her sunny disposition. Rebecca thought happily of her mother whenever Aunt Miriam was around. They both shared the same sunny character and had a way of making you laugh when you were experiencing your greatest pain.

"So good to see you dear!" she examined Rebecca and assessed that her niece had been crying, but decided not to mention it since Rebecca had at least tried to appear cheerful. "I assume your father is in his cave?" she stated with a disapproving look.

"I suppose so," Rebecca shrugged her shoulders.

"I thought I'd take you shopping today, dear! It looks like you could use a new dress for the Derby," Aunt Miriam winked.

"Shopping! Oh, how wonderful! I'd love to get out and go shopping!" Rebecca's eyes twinkled in anticipation. "But I don't think we're going to the Derby this year." Her countenance fell slightly.

"Well, we'll see," Miriam winked. "You run along and get ready to go while I speak with your father for a moment," Miriam nodded toward the stairs.

Rebecca trotted up the staircase and Miriam knocked lightly on the large oak door to Ethan's study. "Ethan, may I come in?" Miriam asked.

"Come," Ethan muttered from the other side. Miriam opened the door wide and strode boldly into the room, a wave of pipe smoke wafted toward her as she entered. Ethan sat behind his desk scribbling on a stack of papers, holding his pipe clenched between his teeth, balancing it lightly with his left hand. He continued writing, barely acknowledging that she had entered the room.

"Hello Ethan! I see you're working hard as usual," she exuded cheerfully.

"Uh hmm," he mumbled without looking up at her.

"Please take a break from that for a few moments and let's talk," she suggested.

Ethan pulled his pipe from his mouth. "I've got a lot to do today, Miriam. I haven't time for one of your lectures," Ethan's voice grew stronger and more authoritative as he glanced up at her and then back to his documents.

Miriam reached over and grabbed the stack of papers and held them in one hand at her side, "The paperwork can wait a minute and I *never* lecture, my dear brother-in-law!"

"Then what do you call it?" he looked up at her expectantly as he held out his hand for her to return his stack of papers.

"I call it conversation – you remember conversation don't you, Ethan? It's that thing people do when they open their mouths, sounds come out and words and messages are conveyed, thoughts shared, and feelings discussed."

He had to admit that her smile and demeanor were enchanting. She reminded him so much of Caroline that he felt that familiar stab in his heart and he suddenly lashed out.

"Miriam, just give me the papers. I have work to do. I don't have time for idle chit chat. Why don't you run along home and hound your own husband?"

"You don't have time for this paperwork, Ethan. Life's too short to spend it holed up in your study working, brooding and letting life pass you by."

"Why not? What's so great about life anyway?" he muttered.

"Why that young girl upstairs! That's what's great about life! Have you gone totally blind?"

He suddenly hung his head, "I – I just don't have it in me anymore, Miriam." He rubbed his temples.

"Rebecca needs a father now more than ever! She's approaching marriageable age and she needs guidance and direction from her father!"

"Rebecca's a good girl. She's got a good head on her shoulders. She's pretty and smart and has a strong faith. She's had enough guidance growin' up to know right from wrong, and she's doin' just fine without me meddlin' in her life."

"Rebecca *is* a good girl. She's all those things you say, but she has no idea about the real world or temptation or the things that a young woman has to deal with at marriageable age. She needs guidance from her father to help her understand what men are like…what men expect."

"If you're talkin' about the whole birds and the bees conversation, her mother had that with her when she turned sixteen, and she's watched enough foals born to know the process," he chuckled at Miriam, ran his fingers through his thick brown hair and leaned back in his chair.

"You know very well what I'm talkin' about, Ethan Marchant! She needs to know about the world, about life. You and Caroline have sheltered her. She's never even been around young men or in social situations. She needs to be introduced to society."

"Introduced to society? What are you drivin' at, Miriam?"

"Rebecca turns seventeen next month and I think she should be given a birthday party with young people as guests so she can be formally introduced to society," Miriam explained.

"Introduced to society – eh? You mean thrown to the wolves!" Ethan stood up. "Caroline and I decided long ago that we wouldn't expose Rebecca to all of that nonsense. We taught her how to work hard, to be self-sufficient, to ride horses, to work on the farm. This nonsense about suitors and bein' launched on society is frivolous and archaic. It's the kind o' thing that makes women into nothin' more than property – objects of men's improper intentions and leads to … well, it leads to no good!"

"Ethan! You can't hide her off in this house and expect Prince Charming to come out of the blue and land on the front porch. You're wasting her prime years. Don't you want her to marry or have children? Don't you want grandchildren, Ethan?" Miriam continued.

"Of course, I want grandchildren. I just think the methods of society are demeaning to women. Women are not objects."

"I agree with you Ethan. Really I totally agree with you. And I'm not saying to throw Rebecca to the wolves. But couldn't we hand-select some young people and invite them to even a small party for Rebecca's seventeenth birthday? What harm is there in that?"

"And who would do the hand-selectin'?" he rubbed his thick brown beard.

"I think we should listen to Rebecca's suggestions about who she would like to invite and we can review the list together."

"All right... but nothin' outlandish," he sat back down and motioned for her to leave the room.

"You've got to be a part of this Ethan. You can't hide off in here in your cave and make me do all the work. You need to be involved in Rebecca's life again. It's time to stop your pity-wallowin' and get out and live again."

"Now don't start on me! It's bad enough that you're meddlin' in Rebecca's life. Don't be hornin' in on mine."

"I'm not hornin' in on your life. But you need to start doin' things with Rebecca again. She's lonely! Can't you see that? For starters, take her to the Kentucky Derby. Take her to the steeplechases. She loves that and misses doing those things with you. Take her for horseback rides at sunset like you used to. Wake up and see the beautiful daughter you have before some young man comes along and takes her away to his own house."

"And I'll have you to thank for that when he does!" Ethan felt that Miriam contradicted herself. One minute she's pushing to socialize Rebecca so she can find a mate and the next she's telling him to spend time with her before someone comes and takes her away.

"Ethan, Rebecca's growin' up. Marriage is inevitable. I'm just tryin' to help her select a suitable companion and I'm tryin' to keep you from wastin' these few precious years you have with her. Can't you wake up and see it?"

"All right, All right, Miriam. Plan the party with Rebecca and I'll try to make myself more available to her." He held out his hand, "Now please give me back my papers."

"Will you take her to the Derby?" Miriam asked.

"Yes, yes, I'll take her to the Derby," he relented.

Miriam plopped the papers on the desk, "Fair enough. But I'm holdin' you to your word."

"Yes, Ma'am" he saluted.

She rolled her eyes, left the room and then a victor's smile spread across her rosy red lips.

Rebecca and Miriam stepped into Mrs. Winesett's dress shop.

"Good mornin', ladies!" the heavy set, middle-aged woman greeted enthusiastically.

"Good mornin', Mrs. Winesett!" Miriam nodded.

"How can I help you ladies?"

"We need a suitable dress and hat for Rebecca to wear to the Derby," Miriam began weaving through the store looking at the dresses.

"Oh, the Derby! I have just the dress!" Mrs. Winesett crossed to the back wall and retrieved a stunning green dress and hat. "I think this one would look lovely with Miss Rebecca's beautiful black hair and dark eyes."

Miriam smiled at Rebecca who nodded in approval.

"You know where the dressing room is, don't you, dear?" Mrs. Winesett handed the dress to Rebecca and pointed.

11

Rebecca took the dress and changed into it. As she stepped out of the dressing room for Miriam to see her, Miriam gasped, "Oh, you look gorgeous in that, Rebecca! You'll be turnin' every young man's head at the Derby for sure!"

"And some older one's as well!" Mrs. Winesett nodded.

Rebecca blushed. Turning men's heads wasn't something she aspired to accomplish. Her mother and father taught her to be proper and respectable and the idea of flaunting herself at a man or adorning herself to capture men's attention seemed shameful.

"Perhaps I need something less… flamboyant?" Rebecca suggested.

"Afraid to turn men's heads, Miss Rebecca?" Mrs. Winesett accurately deduced with a wink.

"I just think it's improper to call such attention to oneself… It's simply immodest …"

"Immodest? Why there's not a thing immodest about that dress, Rebecca! It has a modest neckline and long sleeves. It's completely proper!" Aunt Miriam defended.

"No, I'm not talkin' about the dress being immodest, Aunt Miriam," Rebecca spoke softly. "I just feel it's immodest to wear something with the intention of luring a man's attentions."

"Good grief, Miss Rebecca!" Mrs. Winesett flung her small hand to her bosom. "How do you think we all got a man to marry us if we didn't lure his attentions in some way or 'nother!" She chuckled and Miriam joined in her mirth.

About that time, the bell chimed on the dress shop door as Annette Silverton entered the store with her mother.

"You two talk it over and I'll go help these ladies," Mrs. Winesett suggested, still chuckling to herself as she went to the front of the store to help Annette and her mother.

"Annette needs a new party dress," Mrs. Silverton explained and Mrs. Winsett set about busily searching for the perfect dress for the curly blond-headed, fair complexioned, petite Annette. Rebecca watched them from across the room, trying not to appear obvious in her observations. She'd grown up with Annette. They attended school together. While she had always been friendly and courteous to Rebecca, Rebecca perceived Annette as a complete flirt. Seems as if she always had one young man or another wrapped around her little finger, and to Rebecca baiting men with audacious attire or flirtation bordered on sinful.

"I like the dress, Rebecca. I say we buy it!" Aunt Miriam announced.

"You don't think it's too... too..."

"Alluring?" Aunt Miriam finished for her.

"Well, yes?"

"Rebecca, dear, you're so pretty we could put you in a feed sack and men would still find you alluring!" Aunt Miriam laughed.

"Please, Aunt Miriam!" Rebecca's eyes darted around the store hoping that no one heard her Aunt's remark.

"So have you two ladies decided? Will this be the dress for the Derby?" Mrs. Winesett returned to where they stood.

"Yes, we'll take it," Miriam smiled decisively.

Rebecca descended the stairs in her new green dress and tapped on her father's study door, "Papa are you ready to go?"

Ethan, who had been staring blankly out his study window answered, "Oh, is it time already?"

Rebecca opened the door and stepped into the room, "Yes, it's that time."

Ethan leaned back in his chair and a broad smile broke across his face, "Well, well, Rebecca! Your Aunt Miriam is right. I better start spendin' more time with you before some young man comes along and steals you away!"

"Oh Papa, you're such a tease!" Rebecca rolled her eyes.

Ethan rose from behind his desk and approached her, extending his arm, "I'm not teasin', Rebecca. I'll be surprised if by the time the Derby's over, you don't have some fella askin' me for courtin' privileges."

Rebecca blushed and took her father's arm, "Like I said, you are a merciless tease, Papa."

When they reached the Derby, heads did turn in Rebecca's direction, but she remained oblivious to them. She was too excited to step into the familiar sights, sounds and smells of the race track. Rebecca lived and breathed horses and to spend a day at the Kentucky Derby with her father at her side was to spend a day in heaven.

They stopped by the stable to see Midnight Silhouette, their entry in the Derby. The horse was a beautiful black stallion with a white patch on his nose. Rebecca gently stroked his neck, "You're gonna win for us today, aren't you

14

boy?" Ethan took a moment to speak with the jockey who then climbed atop the horse and started off for the track. Ethan and Rebecca took their seats and waited for the race to start.

Midnight Silhouette got off to a good start and remained neck-and-neck with another horse named Indian Summer throughout the race. Rebecca and Ethan rose to their feet cheering as the horses took their last lap around the track. Rebecca glanced over at her father and chuckled. She was so happy to see him back to his old self as he cheered and clapped excitedly. Even when Indian Summer beat Midnight Silhouette by a nose, she still couldn't keep from smiling as her father pounded his fist into his hand.

"Ah, we almost had 'im! So close!" He took Rebecca by the shoulders and hugged her, "But second place isn't bad, is it? That's the best we've done since Day Star won in '78!" Rebecca and Ethan excitedly made their way over to the horses to congratulate the winner.

"That's quite a horse you have there, Dave," Ethan congratulated Indian Summer's owner, David Phillips.

"And you as well! Ol' Midnight gave our boy a run for the money!"

Rebecca patted Midnight's neck and spoke with the jockey until it was time to present the trophies.

On their way home, Rebecca and her father chatted as if it were old times. It was the first time Rebecca had seen her father relax and be his usual jovial self since her mother's death from the flu eight months prior. She hoped that he was finally snapping out of the haze that had shadowed his spirit.

"Your Aunt Miriam tells me that you two are plannin' a birthday party for next month. Have you decided who you'll be invitin'?"

"Yes, we're inviting about ten people," she nodded. "Thank you for agreeing to it, Papa!"

"Well, thank your Aunt Miriam. She gave me quite a lecture about you needin' to socialize more with young people your own age," he smiled over at her as he held the reins to the team loosely in his hands. "So how many young men and women are you invitin'?"

"Well, it's even - five young men and five young women," she answered.

"Then it's not even, Rebecca. You need another young man," he winked.

"What do you mean?"

"You're forgettin' yourself. You need another young man so that every young man has a young woman," he suggested, his eyes twinkling at his daughter.

"Hmmm.. I don't know who else to invite," she shrugged her shoulders.

"Here, this young man would love an invitation, I'd suspect," he handed her a slip of paper with a man's name and address written on it.

"Who's this?" her eyes expressed her puzzlement.

"That's Dave Phillips' son. He saw you at the winner's circle and asked me if he might come to call on you."

"Oh," Rebecca fumbled nervously with the piece of paper. Her mind searched trying to remember who he was and what he looked like.

"I told you, someone would be askin' me for courtin' privileges before the day was out," he winked.

"I don't even recall a young man at the winner's circle," Rebecca's eyebrows furrowed as she tried to remember.

"Well, he's a few years older than you. He's in his mid-twenties I'd say," Ethan explained.

"Oh, *him?*" Rebecca remembered seeing a man in his twenties standing by Dave Phillips. He was a tall, trim fellow with auburn hair and deep blue eyes. "I suppose we could send him an invitation."

"I take it you weren't too impressed with him?"

"I don't know enough about him to be impressed," she answered truthfully.

Ethan chuckled, "I told Aunt Miriam you were a level headed girl!" He jiggled the reins and the horses increased their gait to a trot.

Something snapped in Ethan on Derby Day. It was as if being planted in the pleasant environment of horse races and jockeys with Rebecca as his companion woke him from a deep slumber and he remembered that there were still things in his life to love. From that day forward, life went back to the way it had been before Caroline's death – or as near as it could be without Caroline's brilliant personality to illuminate the house. Rebecca and Ethan enjoyed their horseback rides at sunset each evening and Ethan began breaking horses and working on the farm again instead of leaving everything to the hired hands. He still refused to sleep in his and Caroline's bedroom and moved into a guest room beside Rebecca's.

The tenth of June, the day of Rebecca's birthday party arrived. Aunt Miriam and her two girls came to help with the decorations. Miriam baked a cake and the girls prepared some punch in the kitchen. Millicent was a seventeen-year-old curly-headed blonde with bright blue eyes and Emily, a fifteen-year-old, had her sister's same fair hair and complexion except her hair was straight instead of curly.

"I'm so excited for you, Rebecca!" Millicent exuded cheerfully as she stirred the punch.

"Me too!" exclaimed Emily.

"Thank you all so much for doing this for me!" Rebecca smiled at them.

Miriam carried the punch into the dining room and placed it on the table next to the birthday cake. "The guests should be arriving soon."

Rebecca wore a burgundy dress that her Aunt Miriam purchased especially for her birthday and she looked striking in it with her black hair and dark eyes. But, Rebecca didn't see her own beauty. She was too busy comparing herself to her cousins and wishing she had their fair complexion and shimmering blonde hair. They were petite – barely five feet tall whereas Rebecca had olive skin, dark hair and eyes and stood five foot eight.

Someone knocked on the front door and Emily scurried to open it. It was Annette Silverton and Beatrice Rodgers. Rebecca really didn't want to invite Annette, but she liked Beatrice and everywhere Beatrice went, Annette followed. They'd been best friends since childhood and if you invited one, you had to invite the other. Ethan stepped into the foyer and helped greet the guests as they arrived.

"Happy Birthday, Rebecca!" Annette and Beatrice chimed in unison.

"Thank you! Thank you for coming," Rebecca greeted as Emily shut the door behind them and another carriage pulled up outside.

"You may as well leave that door open, Emily," Ethan suggested. Guests began arriving and entering the house. Among them was the handsome Stephen Phillips. Upon entering the door, he lifted his hat from his auburn head. He wore a neatly trimmed beard and mustache and his blue eyes twinkled as he took Rebecca's hand and kissed it.

"Happy Birthday, Miss Marchant. Thank you for inviting me."

"Thank you for coming Mr. Phillips," she smiled at the Derby winner's son.

"How are you doing, Sir?" Mr. Phillips greeted Ethan with a firm handshake.

"Very well, very well! And you?" Ethan replied

"Wonderful!" Stephen Phillips answered.

"How's your father doin'? Still starin' at that trophy, I bet?" Ethan chuckled.

Stephen laughed warmly and replied, "Father's doing very well, Mr. Marchant."

Miriam loved to entertain so she began gathering everyone into the dining room, "I'd like to welcome everyone to Rebecca's birthday party. Thank you for coming. First, we'll play a game of croquet in the backyard and then we'll have sandwiches, punch and cake after the game. So if everyone will follow me…" She motioned for the group to follow her out the back door where she and her daughters had set up the croquet course.

Mr. Phillips stayed at Rebecca's side the entire time. His constant presence made the other young men feel that he had already laid claim to Rebecca so they each found their own companion for the afternoon.

"I hope croquet isn't too childish of a game for you, Mr. Phillips," Rebecca offered apologetically thinking a man in his twenties would have no desire for games.

"You're never too old for croquet, Miss Marchant," he smiled as he hit the ball with the mallet and it shot ten feet and sailed through the wicket.

"Good shot!" Rebecca congratulated.

After their game concluded, the party went indoors to enjoy their refreshments. Mr. Phillips' constant companionship made Rebecca a little uneasy. She wasn't used to any young man paying her such rapt attention. While she enjoyed his company and the pleasant conversation, she would have been more comfortable if only girls had been invited to the party.

Mr. Phillips was the last guest to leave. As Rebecca saw him to the door, he pulled a small box wrapped in white paper with a bright red ribbon around it from his pocket. "I brought you a little gift, Miss Marchant."

"How thoughtful of you, Mr. Phillips!" she smiled up into his blue eyes and took the box from his hands. She opened it to find a pair of bright red riding gloves.

"These are lovely. Thank you!" she smiled as her fingers caressed the smooth red velvet.

"I was hopin' you might go ridin' with me tomorrow. You can wear them then," he smiled.

"Tomorrow?" she hesitated and looked to her father who leaned his shoulder against his study door watching Mr. Phillips' departure. Ethan nodded and Rebecca answered, "Yes, I suppose I could do that."

"How does ten tomorrow mornin' sound?" he suggested

"That'll be fine," she agreed.

He stepped out the front door and tipped his hat, "I'll see you tomorrow then, Miss Marchant. Thank you for a lovely afternoon." He turned and walked toward his carriage and Rebecca shut the door.

Immediately Emily and Millicent ran up to her, each one clutching one of her arms in their hands, "Rebecca! I believe the handsome Mr. Phillips is completely smitten with you!" Millicent exuded.

"Oh, I'm sure he was just being nice," Rebecca waved her hand as if it were nothing.

"Surely you're not *that* blind, Rebecca!" Millicent teased. "It's obvious that he's enchanted by you."

"*Enchanted?* Oh, please Millicent! You're always so melodramatic." Rebecca rolled her eyes, set her gloves in their gift box on a table in the foyer and started toward the dining room to help Miriam clean.

"Mother, don't you think Mr. Phillips is completely smitten by Rebecca?" Millicent tugged her mother's arm.

"Oh, yes, it's obvious he's simply enchanted by you!" Miriam smiled at Rebecca and then winked at Millicent.

"You too are just silly!" Rebecca took a handful of dishes into the kitchen and prepared to wash them in a dishpan.

"No, no, Rebecca! No dishes for you today. It's your birthday. The girls and I will take care of that. Go put those beautiful riding gloves from the man who isn't smitten with you in your room," Miriam teased.

As Rebecca left the kitchen Emily called out, "You know that red is the color of love don't you, Rebecca?" Emily, Millicent and Miriam burst into giggles as Rebecca shook her head in frustration and closed her eyes.

Over the next two months, Stephen Phillips became Rebecca's riding companion nearly three times each week. He frequently brought her little trinkets and they became good friends. She enjoyed his company and he helped alleviate some of the loneliness that Rebecca felt from the loss of her mother.

The last morning in August after one of their rides through the Kentucky countryside, Rebecca and Stephen dismounted their horses and tied them to a tree. Stephen extended his arm and Rebecca took it with her gloved hand. He guided her over to a small fishing pond on the West side of the Marchant property.

"Miss Marchant," he turned and took her hands in his, "We've become close over the last couple months, wouldn't you say?"

"Yes, we've become good friends, Mr. Phillips," she nodded.

He reached in his pocket and pulled out a small box. Rebecca's stomach felt queasy. He opened the box and knelt on one knee, still holding her hand in his left hand as he extended the open box to her with his right, "I'd like for us to be more than friends, Miss Rebecca. I'd like… well, what I mean to say is will you marry me?"

Rebecca stood there unable to speak, staring at the full karat diamond engagement ring. She hadn't expected anything like this so soon. While she enjoyed Stephen's company, she saw him only as a friend. He was kind, gentle, and fun. But he felt more like a brother than a lover.

"I – I'm flattered, Mr. Phillips. May I have some time to think on it? Perhaps speak with my father?"

"I did ask your father for your hand and he agreed that I may have it if you are willing to give it." He thought perhaps she didn't realize he'd already asked for her father's permission.

"I'd like a little time to think it over if I may, Mr. Phillips?" she asked again, still staring at the ring in his hand without taking it from him.

Stephen rose to his feet, "Certainly, take all the time you need, but please, take the ring and wear it." He lifted the ring from the box and pulled the riding glove from her left hand and slipped the ring on her finger.

"It's beautiful, Mr. Phillips," she had to admit that. It was the most brilliant diamond she'd ever seen.

"And please, call me Stephen," he looked into her dark brown eyes

She swallowed the nervous lump which had formed in her throat as he leaned forward staring at her lips. Just as his lips would have met hers, Rebecca involuntarily turned her head and his kiss met her cheek. Somewhat embarrassed he pulled back to look into her eyes questioningly.

Nervously, she slipped the riding glove back on her hand and started back to the horses, "I promised my father we'd spend some time together this afternoon. I'll think over your generous proposal Mr. Phillips."

Perplexed, Stephen followed after her, mounted his horse and caught up with her as she rode back to the house.

"Is everything all right?" he finally asked after they'd ridden for nearly five minutes in silence.

"Oh, everything's fine. I'm just thinking," she smiled, hoping he wouldn't read the turmoil within her. What in the world would she tell him? She enjoyed his company and his friendship, but marriage? She didn't want to hurt him, but she also didn't want to marry someone she didn't love. Then again, marrying Stephen made sense. They came from horse breeding families, enjoyed the same things, lived comparable lifestyles and got along well together. But there was just no magic and while Rebecca could be a prude at times, she still held within her heart a longing for heart-pumping, toe-tingling romance. She doubted that would ever be possible with dear sweet Stephen.

When they reached the house, they tied their horses up and Rebecca invited Stephen in for a cool drink, but he declined. "I'll run along now. I have some business to attend to. You will think about my proposal won't you, Miss Rebecca?"

"Yes, I'll think about it. I promise," she smiled and then in an effort to make him feel less uneasy by her aloof reaction to his proposal, she put her hands around his neck, pulled his head forward and kissed his cheek. "Thank you, Stephen, I do so enjoy our time together."

Encouraged, he grinned, mounted his horse and rode away. He assumed that a fine young woman such as Rebecca had never been kissed and that her inexperience had been her reason for turning her cheek when he tried to kiss her earlier.

Ethan met Rebecca as she stepped into the house. She pulled off her riding gloves and laid them on the table.

"I take it you've accepted Mr. Phillips proposal then?" Ethan pointed to the ring on her finger.

"Oh, this?" Rebecca held up her hand. "Can you believe the size of this diamond, Papa?" Rebecca marveled that any man would spend such a fortune on her.

"You're worth it, Rebecca. Of course you don't understand that, but you are." Rebecca wondered how her father seemed to read her thoughts. Ethan approached her and put his hand to her cheek. "So you're going to marry him?"

"I told him I'd think about it. I didn't plan to take the ring but he insisted," she looked up into her father's eyes. "I really would like to talk with you about this. Are you up for that ride we planned to take?"

"Sure, I'd enjoy that," Ethan opened the door for Rebecca, allowing her to step outside and he followed, shutting the door behind them. Rebecca led her horse around to the water trough for a drink while Ethan saddled his horse and prepared to go riding.

The horses traveled at an easy gait for several minutes and Ethan looked over to Rebecca, "So what did you want to talk about?"

"Do you think I should marry Stephen?" she asked.

"It's not my decision to make, sweetie," he stopped his horse and Rebecca turned hers to face him.

"But if it were your decision to make, would you tell me to marry him?" Rebecca pressed.

"Well, do you love him?" he searched her eyes for the truth. Whenever he did that, Rebecca knew that her father could read right through any façade she may put on. So she answered truthfully.

"I don't think so. I care for him as a friend, but I don't feel... there's no...

"Spark?" he finished for her.

"Right, there's no spark. No magic. Is it even realistic to expect that or is that just the stuff from which fairy tales are made? We're definitely no Romeo and Juliet!" she chuckled.

"Well, you wouldn't want to be them anyway, sweetie. Just look how they ended up."

"True, but is it realistic to expect to feel something special or is it just supposed to feel comfortable, like an old well-worn shoe?"

"I'll be honest with you sweetie. In the beginning you usually feel some sparks and then after you're married for a while, it can get more like that well-worn shoe, but it's a shoe that you love and occasionally you'll still feel a spark or two that lets you know there's still a flame burnin'."

"So what you're telling me is that if I don't feel anything special now..."

"I'm not tellin' you anything. Why don't you just think on it a spell? Pray about it and see what kind o' feelin' you get in a few days. Listen to your heart and you'll know what to do."

Rebecca sighed heavily.

"Let's get your mind off it for a spell. I'll race you over to that fence" he pointed to a fence a mile in the distance.

"All right, ready, set, go!" she called and their horses took off at full speed. They were neck-and-neck until about half-way when Rebecca's horse took the lead and she no longer noticed her father coming up alongside her. When she didn't hear his horse's hooves in pursuit, she turned her head to look behind her and saw that his horse had stopped and he lay in a heap on the ground beside it.

Rebecca quickly turned her horse and in lightning speed she had reached her father's side, dismounted and knelt on the ground beside him. "Papa! What's wrong?" She held his head in her lap.

"It's my heart! My arm's killin' me and …" he winced in pain, clutching his chest.

"I'll go for help!"

"No… Rebecca, listen … to … me," he panted. "I should have… Before you decide … anythin'…return to Soquili." He gasped one last breath and sighed in a whisper, "Return to … Soquili."

"Papa, please! Hang on Papa!" tears poured from her dark brown eyes as she knelt there sobbing with her father's head in her lap.

Rebecca stood beside her father's open grave with tears cascading from her cheeks, clutching a handful of rich dirt in her hand. She released it and the soil scattered noisily atop the casket. Stephen put his arm around her pulling her away from the grave. Aunt Miriam and Uncle Dan along with Emily and Millicent gathered around her embracing each other as they wiped tears from their eyes with handkerchiefs.

Into Rebecca's mind drifted her father's dying words, "Return to Soquili." Rebecca lifted her gaze to her aunt. "I must go see Grandma at Soquili."

"What do you mean, Rebecca?" Miriam asked and Stephen studied Rebecca intently.

"Papa's last words to me were 'Return to Soquili.' I must go to Georgia immediately."

"You can't run off to Georgia now, Rebecca. You need time to grieve properly," Stephen insisted.

"No I must go immediately," Rebecca countered.

"What *exactly* did Ethan tell you when he died, Rebecca?" Miriam's brow furrowed with concern.

"He said 'I should have... Before you decide anythin' return to Soquili.' And then he repeated it again 'Return to ... Soquili.' And then he died. Do you know what he meant, Aunt Miriam?"

"Before you decide what? What were you trying to decide?" Miriam asked.

Rebecca looked hesitantly toward Stephen, "We had been discussing Mr. Phillips' marriage proposal, so I think he meant for me to return to Soquili before I decided on the proposal. I just don't understand why. Do you?"

"I have no idea why you'd need to go to Georgia or how that would relate to your decision. I do know that I can't take you to Georgia anytime soon. There's too much to be done on your father's estate and the girls and..." Miriam began.

"No, I don't need you to go with me. I can catch a train straight to Chattanooga and have Grandma pick me up there," Rebecca explained.

"You can't go to Georgia alone, Rebecca! I'll accompany you," Stephen insisted.

"She can't travel with *you*, Mr. Phillips!" Miriam pointed out the impropriety of such a situation.

"I want to go alone. If there's somethin' father should have told me or done that relates to Soquili, I want to discover it for myself... alone," Rebecca turned to her family members, "Could I please have a moment with Mr. Phillips?"

"Certainly dear," Miriam and the others started back toward the house. As soon as they were out of hearing distance, Rebecca pulled the diamond ring from her left hand and handed it to Stephen, "Here's your ring Mr. Phillips. I can't accept it."

"But your father said not to decide until *after* you visited Soquili. Don't turn me down yet. Keep the ring," Stephen refused to take it.

"Please take it, Stephen, for safe keeping at least. I'll wait on my decision, but I can't possibly take such a valuable piece of jewelry with me when I'm traveling alone so far from home."

Reluctantly Stephen took the ring, "All right, but I'm holdin' it for you for when you return. It's yours and my proposal stands."

She patted his arm, "I know, Stephen, but I'll not leave you hanging. As soon as I discover what Papa was tryin' to tell me, I'll make my decision and I'll let you know my answer."

"How long will you be gone?" Stephen's eyes puckered with worry.

"As long as it takes. It may be months. So please don't wait for me. If you need to go on with your life, please don't wait for me."

"I'll wait as long as it takes," Stephen insisted resolutely. "I love you, Rebecca."

"I care a great deal for you too, Stephen." She hugged her friend, burying her head in his shoulder as tears flowed.

He held her in his arms stroking her silky black hair and let her cry on his shoulder until finally he asked, "When will you leave?"

"I'll write Grandma and as soon as I hear back from her, I'll buy my train ticket to Chattanooga. I'll stay with Aunt Miriam until then."

Chapter 2

*G*ray misty fog obstructed Rebecca's view from the carriage window. The driver slowed the conveyance to a snail's pace as he peered through the mist, barely able to see a yard or two ahead of the team. Holding his lantern aloft, the lanky bearded man peered into the vapor as he tugged the reins, bringing the team to a halt.

"Why 're we stoppin', Bert?" huffed Rebecca's uncle, Edmund Marchant, a rotund, balding man in his mid forties.

"It's this blamed fog! I can barely see my hand in front of me," the elderly gray-haired coachman answered as he lightly tapped the reins so that the horses would move forward slowly.

Rebecca continued to stare out into the foggy night and for a moment she imagined that she could see soldiers fighting in the field. She could almost hear their audible screams and gunfire blasts as they attacked each other, locking bayonets and falling to the ground. A cold shiver climbed her spine and she closed her eyes, shaking away the vision.

"What's the matter child? Someone traverse your grave?" it was the first full sentence her uncle had spoken to her since picking her up at the train station in Chattanooga. He peered across the carriage at her as the coach jostled from the ruts in the old dirt road.

"No Sir, but it feels like we may be crossing over someone else's," she gazed out the window as a family of deer lifted their heads to meet her dark brown eyes.

"Ah, you've been listenin' to too many ghost tales. I suppose your parents told you 'bout Old Green Eyes?" he asked flatly. He couldn't get over how much she looked like someone he'd known long ago. Her dark brown eyes, jet black hair, high cheekbones, full lips and olive skin betrayed her Cherokee ancestry.

"No, but they did tell me that Union soldiers lay dead in the Chickamauga battlefield for two months before they finally buried them in groups, standing up in unmarked graves," she turned to look at her uncle. "Who is old Green Eyes? Or dare I ask?"

"Probably shouldn't tell ya. Last thing I need is a child screamin' in the night from nightmares," he put a toothpick in his mouth and picked at his yellowed teeth.

A few stray beams from Bert's lantern softly illuminated the coach and bounced eerie shadows off the mist. Rebecca couldn't help contrast her uncle Edmund with her dear father. Ethan Marchant was a handsome jovial man, but his brother Edmund seemed so homely and emotionless. Both brothers fought for the Confederacy, but after the war Ethan moved to Kentucky while Edmund stayed in North Georgia and continued to run the family's horse farm. Rebecca's father refused to return for a reason unbeknownst to Rebecca so she had never been to Georgia herself. This made her father's dying words even more haunting. "Return to Soquili" he had said. Rebecca wondered how she could return to a place she had never been.

Coming to stay with her bachelor uncle wasn't exactly Rebecca's idea of an ideal place to mend her broken heart. What little she'd heard about her uncle Edmund led her to believe that he would offer her little by way of comfort or compassion. Personally, she sensed no cruelty in the man, but something about him seemed brooding and emotionless.

The one bright spot in Rebecca's world was in knowing that she would be staying at Soquili, the home of her father's youth. She'd heard him tell stories of his childhood and his favorite hiding places. She wished he were here to show her around. She wished he were here just to hug her and let her know that everything would be all right.

Most of all, she looked forward to seeing her dear sweet grandmother Jemima. Jemima visited them in Kentucky four times throughout Rebecca's childhood. She always brought treats and little rag dolls that she made just for Rebecca.

Soquili, which means *horse* in Cherokee, was bordered on two sides by the Chickamauga creek that separated it from the Chickamauga Battlefield. Soquili was basically a bite out of the Southeast side of the battlefield. Named by Jemima Marchant who was half Cherokee, Soquili boasted a thriving horse farm primarily run by slave labor prior to the war. When the slaves were freed, most of them loved the family and the farm so much that they chose to stay on at Soquili as hired hands.

The carriage crossed the rickety Alexander Bridge and Rebecca could hear the swollen waters of the Chickamauga creek below.

"Papa told me that Soquili means horse, but what does Chickamauga mean?" Rebecca asked her uncle.

"It means *river of death*," he answered solemnly.

"Oh," she gulped.

"Seems quite appropriate for what went on here. Ironic that the Cherokees should name it that so many years before the war even took place," her uncle mused as he stared out the window at the ambling creek. Bert turned the coach into a driveway which led to a large plantation house.

While the fog remained, the lanterns from Soquili broke through the soup to illuminate the house. Rebecca breathed in the cool night air and caught the distinctive combination of hay, buckwheat and a hint of horse manure.

"Mother's very excited that you're comin' to stay with us. I travel quite frequently, but Mother'll make you feel welcome I'm sure." It wasn't what he said that seemed so mundane as how he said it. Rebecca wondered if Uncle Edmund would even be able to generate enough inflection in his voice to yell, "The house is on fire!" to stir anyone to action.

The carriage pulled in front of the house and her uncle opened the coach door, stepped out and helped Rebecca down from the carriage. The plantation house stood even larger than she had imagined. At first sight, Rebecca loved the spacious white mansion with its black shutters, huge white columns and vast front porch. She couldn't wait to spend hours chatting with her grandmother in the rockers on the front porch.

Bert pulled Rebecca's trunk from the top of the coach and an elderly black gentleman came from inside the house, taking the other end of the trunk and helping Bert carry it into the house.

As Rebecca ascended the front porch steps, her Grandmother Jemima scurried out onto the porch with her arms wide, "My little Rebecca! My, how you've grown into such a beautiful young woman!" Jemima embraced her granddaughter fondly and then pulled her back examining her from head to toe. Jemima looked a bit older than Rebecca remembered – a few more wrinkles. But she was still as beautiful. Her dark hair grayed at the temples and her high cheekbones accentuated her beautiful brown eyes. "My, my Rebecca! The next doll I'll be makin' you will be for one of your youngins! You're plum grown! How old are you now? Seventeen?"

"Yes, Ma'am, I'll be eighteen in June."

"That's right!" Jemima led her granddaughter into the spacious entryway. The vaulted ceiling and the elaborate staircase provided such grandeur that Rebecca felt like pinching herself to make sure she wasn't dreaming.

"Bert and Jefferson carried your trunk upstairs. Follow me, dear, and I'll show you to your room." Jemima put her arm around Rebecca's shoulder, giving her a tight squeeze, "I'm just so thrilled to have you here with us!"

"I'm happy to see you again, Grandma!" Rebecca just wished that the reunion had been under happier circumstances.

Noting the hint of sadness in her granddaughter's eyes, Jemima put her hands on Rebecca's shoulders and turned her to face her, "I'm so sorry that the last year has just been so horrible for you, dear!" Rebecca fell into her grandmother's embrace and brushed a tear from her eye with the back of her hand.

"Come along," Jemima took Rebecca's hand and led her up the staircase and down the corridor. "Perhaps this will cheer you up a bit," she winked. Jemima opened the door to the most amazing bedroom Rebecca had ever seen. A large full size oak canopy bed draped with beautiful forest green tapestries first caught her attention on the left side of the room. Her eyes worked their way around the room to a night table by the bed, an oak chest of drawers along the far wall and a window ornamented with matching green drapes and valence. A cozy fire roared in the fireplace across from the bed and an oak dresser stood along the wall by the door.

"It's gorgeous!" Rebecca's dark brown eyes widened.

"Looks like they put your trunk there at the foot of the bed," Jemima pointed. "Go ahead and change out of your travel clothes and wash up. And please, don't be wearin' black. I just can't bear the sadness of black. There's a basin of fresh water and towels over here on the dresser. When you're ready come on downstairs and eat somethin'. Hilda 'll have dinner ready soon."

"Thank you, Grandma!" Rebecca called as Jemima turned and left the room, shutting the oak door behind her.

Rebecca crossed to the night table and adjusted the wick of the lamp to better illuminate the room. She examined everything, lingering at the dresser and picking up a small picture frame. It was her father, mother and herself as a baby. She couldn't have been more than a year old when it was taken. She'd never seen the photograph before and gently ran her finger along the tin type and returned it to its place on the dresser.

She opened her trunk and removed a burgundy dress, laying it out on the bed. After changing out of her travel clothes, she washed up and stared at her reflection in the large ornate mirror that hung over the dresser. Rebecca despised her appearance. Totally oblivious to her own striking beauty she wished that she had curly blonde tresses and fair skin like Millicent instead of her sleek thick black hair and olive complexion. She straightened a few loose braids, dressed and descended the stairs. Once in the foyer, she looked around trying to determine which direction led to the dining room.

"This way Miss Marchant," Jefferson smiled, nodded and motioned her toward the right. "The dining room is through here." He looked back over his shoulder at her and shook his head as if he were trying to make sense of something. Rebecca puzzled at his expression but followed the elderly butler through the heavy oak double doors that led into a spacious living room and adjoining dining room. A small fire burned in the fireplace and Jemima and Edmund already sat at the dining room table.

"Rebecca! Don't you look lovely in that burgundy dress!" Jemima smiled and Edmund, who sat at the head of the table, rose as she approached. Jefferson pulled out the chair across from Jemima and Rebecca sat down.

"It's your house that's lovely, Grandma! Papa told me it was big, but he never told me how grand it was!" Rebecca gazed up at the crown molding on the twelve-foot ceilings.

"I 'spect that your Papa was too busy traipsin' through hollers and marshes and fishin' in the creek to notice such things," she winked. "Ain't that right, Edmund? You boys were always runnin', ridin' and huntin' outdoors."

"I guess we were," Edmund nodded almost imperceptibly. Rebecca couldn't imagine her uncle having enough gumption to run, ride or hunt.

"They ran around playin' like they were Cherokee braves, huntin' deer and trappin' rabbits. It was a chore to pull 'em indoors long enough to eat. And gettin' 'em to bathe was nigh to impossible!" Jemima laughed.

"Please mother," Edmund rolled his eyes.

"Don't mind Edmund, dear. He's plum forgot what it's like to be young. He hasn't known what that was like for nigh onto eighteen years – ever since ..." Jemima stopped herself and suddenly became somber as she raked her fork through her plate and shoved a helping of mashed potatoes in her mouth.

"What Mother is trying to say, Miss Rebecca, is that war changes people. You can't see that kind of death, carnage and heartbreak and still laugh about such frivolous things anymore. You wake up to the real world when you endure somethin' like that," Edmund put a piece of pork chop in his mouth and chewed.

"Is that why Papa never came back to Georgia? Did it bring back too many horrific memories?" she thought aloud.

"Uh, suppose so, among other things," Edmund mumbled and Jemima continued to fiddle with her food.

"Enough of this dark talk, let's think on somethin' lighter!" Jemima suddenly offered cheerfully. "Tomorrow, you take that black stallion and ride around the property. I know you'll fall in love with the place once you get a chance to see it in daylight."

"I'm sure I will," Rebecca smiled.

"You ever cross-stitch, dear?" Jemima asked.

"Sometimes," Rebecca nodded.

"I'm workin' on a piece and almost have it finished. It's a scene of the creek that runs along the backside of our property. I thought I'd try to finish it tonight. If you'd like I'll give you some material and thread and you can join me, and we'll chat and catch up on things."

"I'd love to," Rebecca smiled. She felt so grateful to be with her grandmother. Rebecca knew that if anyone could help drive away the dark gloomy cloud that seemed to hang over her, Grandma Jemima could.

Edmund suddenly rose from his seat and tossed his napkin into his chair, "Well, I'll leave you two women to chit chat and sew. I'm goin' to my study to read." Without waiting for a reply he strode toward the living room and out the double doors.

"Is he always so happy-go-lucky?" Rebecca giggled.

"Oh, always, absolutely!" Jemima chuckled, putting her hand over her mouth. "On the bright side, nothing rattles him, but on the sad side," Jemima's face suddenly fell, "he never knows joy."

"How sad! What happened to him?" Rebecca whispered.

"He… uh… he lost someone very dear to him at the end of the war and he's never been the same since," Jemima confided.

"Oh really? Was uncle Edmund married?"

"No, he never married. But we mustn't speak of it further," Jemima whispered and instantly changed the subject. "Do you still enjoy riding? You were doing so well with it the last I saw you – jumpin' fences and competin' in shows. Your father did a fine job of trainin' you!"

"I still ride, but I haven't competed since…well, since Mama died," Rebecca fiddled with the last bite of food on her plate and then set her fork down. Rebecca wondered if Uncle Edmund had lost someone he loved as dearly as her father loved her mother.

"Are you finished, Miss?" Hilda, one of the freed slaves who stayed on as a servant, asked Rebecca.

"Yes, Ma'am, thank you very much," Rebecca turned to look up at the woman whose eyes widened and she dropped a fork causing it to clang loudly on the floor.

"I'm sorry, Ma'am," the woman nodded nervously at Jemima and stooped down to pick up the fork from the hardwood floor. The slightly over-weight, middle-aged woman seemed to gain her composure, "We're happy to have you with us, Miss. I know Mrs. Marchant will enjoy havin' your bright company." She nodded and took Rebecca's plate quickly to the kitchen.

"Is she all right?" Rebecca asked puzzled.

"She's just been a bit jittery today. She's probably embarrassed that she dropped somethin' the first time she met you," Jemima waved her hand as if it were of no concern.

"Oh," Rebecca wasn't sure she believed that was the reason because the woman looked shocked before she even dropped the fork. But Rebecca could tell by her grandmother's expression that she shouldn't press it. So

Rebecca rose from her seat, "I'd love to see your cross stitch, Grandma."

Jemima stood and Rebecca followed her over to a plush wingback chair with a sewing basket next to it. She opened the basket and unfolded a realistic cross stitch of the wooded creek, "Here it is."

"Oh, that's just beautiful!" Rebecca reached out to examine the stitches. "You do such meticulous work, Grandma! I'm afraid I'm not near so talented." Rebecca shook her head.

"Oh, it just takes havin' too much time on your hands," Jemima chuckled.

"Well, I guess I'll have plenty of that now," Rebecca observed.

Jemima let Rebecca rummage through her sewing basket and select items to begin her own cross stitch. They talked, laughed and sewed until it got so late that Rebecca could hardly keep her eyes open.

"I'm sorry, Grandma, but I'm just too tired to see these small stitches any longer," Rebecca dropped her sewing to her lap.

"Oh, I'm the one who's sorry, dear! You've had a long trip and I've kept you up too late." She extended her hands, "Here, let me put that up for you and you run along to bed. When you're up in the mornin' just come down and Hilda will have a nice breakfast ready for you."

Rebecca stood, handed the sewing to her grandmother and leaned over to kiss her cheek and hug her goodnight.

"Sweet dreams, dear," Jemima's kind eyes wrinkled with her happy smile.

"Thank you. You too," Rebecca turned and went upstairs to bed.

Hundreds of bloodied and mangled bodies littered the ground. Their anguished groans rent the air and shrill screams came from the little cabin on the hill. The pungent stench of death and gunpowder filled her nostrils.

"Help me, Miss!"

She screamed as she felt a tight grip clutching frantically at her ankle. She looked down at the Union soldier's bloody face. His shoulder bled profusely as he gasped, "Please, Miss, help me!"

"I... I'm sorry, I'm not a nurse," she stammered as her heart raced and she instinctively attempted to free her ankle from his grasp.

"Please, I'm so thirsty! Do you have some water?"

She looked around and found a canteen lying on the ground a few feet away. Lifting the soldier's head, she held the canteen to his lips. She peered around the battle ground looking for someone who could help the man.

"Over here!" she called to two Union soldiers carrying a stretcher as they searched among the wounded. "This man's still alive over here! Can you please help him?"

The two men stepped over bodies carrying a stretcher toward her.

"Thank you, Miss," a dark haired Union soldier smiled as they lifted the man onto the stretcher.

"What are you doing out in the middle of this God-forsaken place?" the blonde-headed soldier asked.

"Uh, I'm lookin' for someone," she stammered.

"Who is it? Maybe we know him," the dark-haired soldier offered.

"Lieutenant Anderson of the third Kentucky," she answered.

"Oh, I don't know him. Do you?" the soldier turned to his companion.

"No, but the third Kentucky was fighting right over there at the crest of the hill," the blonde soldier pointed to his right.

"Thank you!" she hurried along, trudging up the embankment to the crest of the hill. There among the dead and dying lay the man she searched for, "Oh Grant!" she exclaimed as tears poured from her eyes and she knelt on the ground beside the wounded soldier. Blood saturated his chest and he groaned in immense pain.

"It's you, my love!" he gasped, his pale steel blue eyes locking into hers. "I thought I'd never see you again."

"Oh Grant, what's happened to you!" she lovingly caressed his face with her soft hand and brushed aside a lock of his brown hair.

He put his hand to hers, "You know I love you, don't you?"

"Of course and I love you!" she whispered and leaned over to softly kiss his parched lips. As she pulled back from him he gazed into her eyes, smiled and exhaled as he lost consciousness.

"Hold on Grant!" she cried hot tears and embraced his broken body carefully. Raising her head, she searched the hillside and field below her for someone who could help.

"Over here!" she called as she waved her hands, "Please help us over here!" she cried out to the same two men who had carried off the other soldier.

Rebecca bolted upright in her bed, sobbing bitterly and gasping for breath. Disoriented, her eyes darted around the room as she struggled to remember where she was. Her eyes caught hold of the low flame of the fire in front of her. She put her hands to her face, wiped the tears from her eyes, and ran her fingers through her thick black hair. Leaning over she turned up the flame on the lamp.

Rebecca had never dreamed anything so vivid. She felt as if she were the young woman rummaging through the battlefield looking for her lover. She stepped out of bed and put another log on the fire, unable to shake the cold scene of death. Knowing that she wouldn't be able to sleep, she pulled a Bible from the night table and read until the dream faded and her eyes grew heavy.

"How was your night, dear?" Jemima smiled as Rebecca sat down at the kitchen table across from her.

"Oh, uh, the bed is very comfortable and I love my room," Rebecca didn't feel like discussing her dream which still weighed heavily upon her mind.

"I'm glad you like it," Jemima smiled.

After breakfast, Jemima suggested that Rebecca take a ride around the property. Rebecca changed into her riding clothes and Jemima led her out to the stables.

"Here, take Midnight. He's a gentle one, but he's got lots of spirit. You'll enjoy ridin' him," Jemima suggested.

"Thank you. He's beautiful!" Rebecca patted the sleek black stallion's snout. So his name is Midnight? We have a Midnight Silhouette that we entered in the Derby this year. He took second place.

"Yes, the two horses share the same ancestry," Jemima explained. "Your Papa took one of the horses from Soquili to breed in Kentucky."

"Oh, I never knew that," Rebecca was surprised her father never told her this.

"Take a ride up that hill and from there you'll see a beautiful meadow that stretches to the Chickamauga Creek that borders our property. On the other side of the creek is the battlefield.

"Thank you. It's a perfect day for a ride," Rebecca studied the clear autumn sky as a gusty breeze blew through the stable.

"Take your time and enjoy yourself," Jemima called as she strode back toward the house.

Rebecca put the bridle on the stallion and strapped on his saddle, then led him out of the stable. Mounting him, she gently nudged Midnight's ribs and he took off at a trot toward the hill. Effortlessly the strong animal ascended the steep wooded hill and Rebecca pulled the reins for him to slow down. Scaly bark hickory trees covered the hill and limestone rocks jutted above the grass and brush. She stopped the horse and beheld the most breathtaking view of rolling meadow sprawling before her with mountains in the distance. The meadow seemed to beckon her, and she nudged Midnight's sides and galloped onward.

Rebecca rode so fast that her ponytail came loose and her dark hair flowed in the wind. She and Midnight made quite a pair for Rebecca's hair was the same jet black color of the stallion. She abruptly pulled the reins as they reached the creek and halted to enjoy the view.

Into her mind flashed images of gray and blue uniforms fighting on the far bank of the creek. She could hear shots fire, the boom of cannons in the distance, groaning and painful screams as wounded men tumbling into the crimson creek water. She almost caught the scent of gunpowder in the air.

"You must be Mrs. Marchant's granddaughter."

Rebecca jumped and her head spun around toward the deep masculine voice. Flinging her hand to her bosom she gasped, "Oh, you scared me to death!" Her pulse raced as she stared at the broad-shouldered, blonde rider atop a calico horse. The handsome stranger who appeared to be in his mid-twenties wore a plaid shirt rolled up to his elbows and his muscular arms held the reins loosely. His gray-blue eyes peered into Rebecca's.

"I'm sorry, Miss. My name is Mitch Garrison," he eased his horse up alongside hers and tipped his hat. "I break the horses for your uncle."

"Oh, I'm Rebecca Marchant," she nodded.

"I figured you would have heard my horse approaching. I didn't mean to startle you. Is everythin' all right? You seemed a bit... distracted."

"I'm fine. I was just thinking about…something," she stared back at the creek.

"You can almost see 'em there, can't ya?" his low voice nearly whispered.

Rebecca's head turned quickly back toward the handsome horseman, "Who?"

"The soldiers. Sometimes when I'm out here, I can almost see 'em fightin' there on the banks o' the creek, their wounded bodies fallin' into the bloody water."

"Yes!" she agreed in shock that he would have experienced the same phenomenon. "That is *exactly* what I was just thinking!"

"It's a shame that such carnage should taint such a beautiful place. But if you can put all that out o' your mind, you'll come to love it for its beauty and you'll forget the horror of its history."

"I hope you're right," she mumbled. She wanted to love this place and certainly didn't want to stay somewhere that constantly provided visions of death and carnage. But so far, Soquili had only offered her vivid visions and dreams of the conflict fought nearby.

"Come on, I'll show ya around," he offered. There was something about him she instantly liked. His friendly eyes and dimpled smile made her feel at home for the first time since she'd arrived at Soquili. He was the only person who didn't have an odd expression in his eyes when he looked at her. She nudged Midnight to follow him.

"The creek runs all along here. It's a beautiful place to swim in the summer months and that little knoll over there makes a great picnic spot. Then if you follow the creek in this direction it takes you over into this low-lyin' area." He led her along the creek back toward the house. "In spring it rains so much the creek floods all o' this and it flows out into the field out to the road. Fortunately, the house and stables are on high enough ground that it doesn't flood them.

"How unusual!" she remarked.

When it floods like that you find all kinds of bizarre things. You can walk out into the field and find fish flappin', strugglin' for air 'cause the water's receded and left 'em in little puddles on the ground.

"Poor things!"

"Makes for easy fishin' though," his chuckle was low and deep. "Last year, we found two calves washed up into the field."

"Did they drown?"

"Nope, they were partially decayed. Mr. Nobles buried 'em back in the field and the rains dredged 'em up and carried 'em out here.

"How gruesome!"

"It was a nasty mess to clean up!" he lifted his hat, ran his hand through his thick blonde hair and replaced his hat. "So I hear you're quite a rider?"

"Oh, I think my grandmother exaggerates," Rebecca shook her head modestly.

"Well, why don't we see? I've got some steeples set up down here," he pointed back toward the field that lay alongside the house and stables.

She followed him back around to the open field. "You start here and then work your way around to the left and back," he pointed to the steeples that he had arranged out in the field.

"Did you set all this up just for yourself?" she asked.

"No, I give ridin' lessons to some of the people who board their horses here," he answered.

"Oh, that's fun! I didn't know Soquili offered riding lessons," she smiled.

"Yep, that's part o' my job," the dimples in his cheek deepened with his smile. "Wanna show me what you can do?"

"If you insist," she smiled. He wouldn't need to twist her arm for she loved the steeples. Nudging Midnight's ribs firmly she took off toward the first hurdle. She jumped each one quickly and easily, clearing each hurdle perfectly without so much as a graze, her black hair blowing in the autumn breeze.

As she came back around to where he still sat atop his horse, he scratched his head, "Maybe you need to be teachin' the classes."

She chuckled, "Oh, I'm sure no one would hire a woman trainer."

"Well, ya never know!" he nodded. "Where'd ya learn to ride like that?"

"My father taught me. He was a horse breeder in Kentucky and raised prize winning race horses. We had one that even won the Kentucky Derby."

"That's impressive!"

"It was a lot of fun," she smiled as she thought back upon her childhood riding horses with her father and mother.

"Let's see some more," he nodded for her to ride again. As the stallion galloped out into the field, Mitch marveled at the striking beauty of the young woman who could ride so well. Something about her looked familiar. He couldn't quite put his finger on where he'd seen her before, but he knew he wanted to get to know her better.

As Rebecca rode back around, she stopped her horse in front of his, "Now it's your turn."

"I'm sorry," he pointed back to the stables, "My next student just arrived. But I have some free time tomorrow mornin'. Would you like a tour of the battlefield? I can tell you the history. Means so much more that way, otherwise you're just lookin' at landscape."

"Sure," Rebecca wanted to see everything, but the eerie feelings she kept experiencing filled her with uncharacteristic trepidation. Having a companion with whom to explore the historical countryside felt safer. "It would be nice to have the company," she nodded.

"All right, meet me around nine at the stables," his straight white teeth flashing a handsome grin, he turned to ride away. Rebecca observed him as his horse galloped back to the stables. He dismounted, tied up the horse and shook a tall dark-haired man's hand. Mitch disappeared into the stables and returned with a pony. He lifted a curly blonde child onto the pony and led her into a fenced field as her father watched. The scene reminded Rebecca of the first time she ever rode a horse and how her father helped her feel safe and secure by leading the animal around by the reins and steadying her with his hand - just as Mitch did for this little girl. She smiled at the memory, but then felt a stabbing ache knowing that her father would never be there to offer her comfort and security again.

She nudged Midnight's ribs and galloped off toward the hill. Mitch's eyes followed her as she passed, ascended the hill and disappeared over the crest, her black hair flowing in the breeze. Rebecca stopped at the top and dismounted. She looped Midnight's reins around a nearby scaly bark hickory tree, gathered a handful of nuts from the base of it and searched among the limestone for a rock that would make a good hammer. Venturing forward, Rebecca sat down next to a large limestone bolder that jutted above the grass.

She folded her legs in front of her, dropped the nuts into her lap and selected one. Holding it steady on the bolder, she tapped the nut with the rock in her right hand until it cracked. She marveled at how much meat filled the hard shell. Most hickory nuts she'd seen were hardly worth the time or effort to open. It took quite a bit of work to extricate the tasty meat from the folds of hard shell. While it tasted similar to a pecan, it certainly wasn't as easy shelling. Rebecca sat for nearly an hour tapping the small round nuggets of nature and enjoying the treasure within. She tried to see how big of a piece she could extricate at one time, and felt a thrill whenever she managed to pull one out in its most complete form. Finally, she gathered up a handful of unshelled nuts and put them in her apron pocket to carry back to the house with her. She remembered seeing a nutcracker in the living room and figured the job would be easier with the right tools.

Rebecca climbed higher up the hill where she'd tied Midnight, loosened him and mounted. Carefully descending the wooded and rocky ridge, she saw Mitch with another student – this time a teenage boy. She waved as she galloped past him and he nodded, tipping his hat. After taking Midnight back to his stall, she removed his bridle and saddle and brushed him down. She loved brushing a horse's mane. There was something soothing and relaxing about it and it made her feel a little bit more at home in her new surroundings.

When Rebecca reentered the house, she caught the distinct delicious aroma of Hilda's creations and went straight for the kitchen.

"Somethin' smells delicious!" she exclaimed as she entered to find Hilda pulling a pumpkin pie from the oven. "Pumpkin pie! I thought those were only for holidays," her big brown eyes widened.

"Every day is a holiday with you here," Jemima answered as she entered from the other side of the kitchen.

"You do know how to make a girl feel welcome, Grandma! And you too Miss Hilda. Thank you so much! I love pumpkin pie!" Rebecca looked around and noticed that Hilda had also made fried chicken, biscuits, mashed potatoes and corn on the cob. "Can I help with anything?"

"No thank you, Miss. I believe everythin's under control," Hilda smiled.

"Let me go wash up and I'll help you set the table. I like to make myself useful and I feel like I've done nothin' but play all mornin'," Rebecca rolled up her sleeves and washed her hands in a nearby basin.

"Thank you, Miss," a young person willing to work impressed Hilda.

"You don't have to do that, Rebecca," Jemima told her as Rebecca went to the cupboard to pull down some plates.

"Oh, I want to Grandma. Put me to work or before long I won't be fit for nothin'," she winked. "That's what Mama always said anyway – idle hands are the devil's workshop."

Rebecca carried the dishes through the swinging door and into the dining room.

"She's a fine young woman, Ma'am. Puts me so much in the mind of..."

"I know, it is uncanny, isn't it?" Jemima shook her head.

Rebecca reentered the kitchen, "Where do you keep the silverware, Miss Hilda?"

"Right over there, Miss, in that drawer," she pointed.

Jemima watched her granddaughter as she left the room again.

"Are you ever gonna tell her, Ma'am?" Hilda whispered.

"Her parents didn't want her to know. I wouldn't want to betray the dead," Jemima shook her head as she whispered her reply.

"Well, pardon me ma'am, but they aren't the only dead to be betrayed," Hilda bit her lip for she knew she'd said too much.

Jemima darted a silencing look, letting the servant know that the discussion had ended. Jemima scooped up a handful of cloth napkins and met Rebecca at the door as she started to reenter the kitchen, "Here, dear, here's some napkins." Jemima accompanied her granddaughter into the dining room. Soon, Hilda followed, both hands carrying drinking glasses.

After they had set the table, Jemima pulled out a chair and sat down.

"What about Uncle Edmund?" Rebecca asked as she placed her hand on a chair and pulled it back.

"Oh, he'll be along later. He's out runnin' errands. We'll save him a plate." Jemima gestured for Rebecca to be seated.

Midway through lunch, Jemima changed the subject abruptly, "So I see you've met our Mr. Garrison." Jemima winked and for some unknown reason, Rebecca felt the blood rush to her face.

"Oh, yes, the trainer," Rebecca shook her head.

"He's a handsome one, don't you think?"

"I suppose so… seems like a nice enough man," Rebecca shrugged her shoulders.

"You suppose so? Why you aren't female if you don't find that man irresistible to look upon!" Jemima chuckled.

Rebecca couldn't hold back the smile any longer. Her Grandma had such a way of lightening her mind. "Ok, yes, he's very handsome Grandma," Rebecca conceded.

"You should ask him to show you around the battlefield. He knows a lot about the history and where all the fightin' took place. His father fought in the war and taught him a lot," Jemima bit into a fried chicken leg.

"He already offered. We're goin' in the mornin'," Rebecca answered.

"I had a feelin'…" Jemima smiled knowingly.

"What?" Rebecca sighed. She knew her grandmother was up to something. She just didn't know what.

"I had a feelin' that young man would jump to your company like a chicken on a June bug!" she laughed.

"Oh please, Grandma! Offerin' to show me around the battlefield is hardly…"

"Sure, sure!" Jemima nodded her head, raising her hand to stop Rebecca's attempt at protest.

"Grandma!" Rebecca was totally embarrassed now but she couldn't help but chuckle at her Grandmother's delightful teasing.

"Seriously, Rebecca. He's a fine young man. He's worked here as a trainer for five years now. He even helped out as a stable boy when he was just a youngin'. He's a hard worker and extremely trustworthy. Interesting, talented, handsome – quite a catch for any young lady," she winked.

"Are you tryin' to marry me off my first full day here?" Rebecca teased.

"No, dear. But I can't help it that I'm a hopeless romantic," the old woman's eyes twinkled. "I'd woo him myself, but I'm afraid I'm a might too old." Jemima broke into a hearty laugh.

"You are the funniest thing, Grandma! I have missed you!" Rebecca joined in her Grandma's mirth.

"What you girls gigglin' about?" Edmund's dry voice boomed as he entered the room.

"Oh nothin' Edmund. Nothin' you'd find the least bit interestin'," Jemima bit her lip and settled down. "Rebecca and I were just finishing up our lunch so we'll leave you to enjoy yours undisturbed." Jemima rose from her seat and motioned for Rebecca to follow her.

Jemima took Rebecca's hand and led her out onto the spacious front porch, sat down on a rocker and patted the arm of the one next to her for Rebecca to join her.

"I bet you're wishin' this porch faced in the other direction so you could enjoy a better view of that handsome horseman," Jemima winked.

"Please Grandma, you're embarrassin' me! Let's talk about somethin' else." Rebecca decided to change the subject herself, "So how long has Hilda worked for the family?"

"She's been with us for nearly thirty-five years. She and Jefferson stayed on with us after the war when they were freed. We had about a half-dozen servants who stayed. Most are still with us. Only a couple have moved on over the years."

"That speaks a lot for the family if they chose to stay when they didn't have to," Rebecca mused aloud.

"We always treated 'em like they belonged here. Really, there's not much different now that they're considered free. We gave 'em a little spendin' money before the war and they still get room, board and pay now," Jemima explained.

Rebecca and Jemima rocked on the front porch, enjoying each other's company for several hours. Jemima enlightened her about her father as a child and Rebecca told Jemima about him as an adult. As they compared experiences, Rebecca gained a better understanding of her father and realized that he hadn't really changed a whole lot. The father she knew embraced life, enjoyed nature and his family. He wasn't far from the little boy her grandmother described. Knowing her father like she did made her feel incredibly sorry for her uncle Edmund who held everything in reserve and never knew true joy or happiness.

After a long and pleasant day, Rebecca settled down for the night in her bedroom. She changed into her nightgown and put another log on the fire, dimmed the lamp and climbed underneath the fluffy green comforter. Snuggling her head into her pillow, she drifted off to sleep.

The handsome soldier's pale steel blue eyes gazed lovingly into hers. She inhaled the sweet aroma of fresh hay and could feel the hay stabbing into her arms and back as she lay in the loft beside him. She could feel her hands on his warm smooth chest and sighed as he leaned over and kissed her lips, running his fingers through her jet black hair. Suddenly she felt him being torn from her embrace. In horrified humiliation she watched as a stocky man stood on the ladder leading to the loft and yanked her soldier, sending him plummeting downward onto a mound of hay.

"Keep your hands off her!" the stocky man bellowed in anger. "Get down from there you trollop!" he turned his familiar brown eyes toward her as he ran his right hand in frustration through his straight thinning black hair. "I can't believe you'd do such a thing! You know better than this, girl!" he seethed. He reached over and grasped the soldier's belongings from the loft and flung them down at him. He directed his words at the soldier who scrambled to his feet, thrusting an arm into his shirtsleeve, "I'd beat you senseless right here if I didn't know that it takes two to play this game!" Turning his head back toward her, his eyes bored through her.

"It's not like you think. I love him!" she vainly attempted to defend her actions.

The stocky man stepped down from the ladder. "You sicken me!" he stared at her with such disdain that she felt as if she were a harlot about to be stoned. "Get in the house" he demanded.

She ran her fingers through her hair attempting to remove the twigs of hay and descended the ladder. The man took her companion by the throat, "You better do right by her, ya hear!"

"Of course I will. I always intended to..." the handsome soldier's eyes followed her as she left the stable and looked pitifully back over her shoulder to meet his gaze. Tears of humiliation streamed down her face as she bolted toward the house.

Rebecca wiped the tears from her cheeks as a horribly intense weight of guilt shrouded her soul. It felt as if she herself had committed such an excessive act of passion. Sitting upright in her bed, she mumbled, "It was just a dream. I didn't do anything wrong. It was just a dream." She tried to shake away the immense guilt which eventually transformed into relief and gratitude that the humiliating event had only been a dream and not a reality. At last she vowed to herself that she would never commit such a sin for the horrible aftermath would never be worth the momentary pleasure.

Chapter 3

Rebecca pulled her shawl around her shoulders as the crisp morning air sent a chill through her body. She opened the stable door and entered. Peering around, she noted the hayloft to the right. Without thinking she approached the ladder and started climbing. Standing on the third rung, she stared at the familiar spot as the dream came flooding back and thick emotions filled her chest, making it difficult to breathe.

"What cha doin'?" Rebecca's head spun around to see Mitch standing in the doorway.

"Oh," she backed down the ladder. "I was just lookin' around." Upon reaching the ground she turned to face him. While she felt extremely attracted to him, something inside her breathed a sigh of relief that he bore no resemblance to the soldier in her dream. She opened the stallion's stall and picked up the bridle.

"Need some help with that?" he offered.

"No thanks, I've got it," she shook her head and slipped the bridle on the horse's snout. Mitch opened the calico's stall and saddled the horse. Neither of them said a word as they girded the saddles on their horses.

"Pretty mornin', don't ya think?" Mitch finally broke the nervous silence.

"Yes, lovely," she agreed.

"You ready?" he asked as he led his horse out of the stall.

"Ready," she led Midnight from his stall and the pair walked side by side out of the stable.

They each climbed atop their horses and Mitch asked, "Where to first?"

"I want to see you run the steeples," she smiled, finally feeling more herself again, having shaken the dream from her mind.

"Oh, I might embarrass myself," he feigned humility. "Or I might be out of a job when you see that you're a better rider than I am."

"I seriously doubt that," she rolled her eyes.

Their horses trotted alongside one another to the field and then Mitch gave his horse a swift kick and the animal took off toward the hurdles, jumping them with ease and grace.

Upon completing the course, Mitch rode back to her.

"I think your job is safe, Mr. Garrison," she smiled.

"Think so – huh?" he grinned. "You ready for the tour?"

"Lead on," she pointed.

Mitch and Rebecca rode side by side out to the main road and turned left. The horses trotted along the road, around the curve, and their hooves clomped across Alexander Bridge. Rebecca looked down at the creek where cows bathed themselves in the water. Along the way Mitch explained about the battle and how it progressed at the various points they passed.

As Alexander Bridge Road met Lafayette Road, they crossed over Lafayette and wound their way back through a wooded path.

"This next place is the Snodgrass house. Thousands died here in this field and on the hill in one of the bloodiest points in the battle. We actually just passed the anniversary of this battle. It was fought September 18th through the 20th and the fighting here at Snodgrass Hill took place on the last day," Mitch explained.

A strange tingle sent a cold shiver up Rebecca's spine, and she gasped audibly as they came through the clearing to the field. The hill with the cabin on the right stood before them.

"What is it?" he asked, staring at her shocked expression, her eyes widened and her mouth dropped open.

"I... I've seen this place before," she mumbled.

"Really? I thought you'd never been to Georgia before?" his eyebrows puckered questioningly.

"I dreamed about this place the first night I came here," she whispered.

"Really? What did you dream?" he asked.

She shook her head nervously, "No, you'll think I'm crazy." But she couldn't help but relive the dream in her mind's eye.

"Tell me, Miss Marchant. I'll believe you," she met his gaze and something told her he really would believe her. But she still hesitated.

"Why would you believe me? You don't even know me." she asked perplexed.

"People have dreams about the battle. They see things around here. It's not uncommon," he reassured. "Tell me. Maybe I can help you make sense of it."

"It must have been the evening after the battle had ended. The sun was setting and it grew dusk. In my dream, I searched among the wounded and the dying. I could smell the gunpowder and the stench of death. Blood curdling screams came from the cabin and men groaned in pain all around me. I was looking for a Union soldier... Lieutenant Grant Anderson." She nudged her horse and trotted over to a spot where she stood eyelevel to where she'd found Grant's body in her dream. Mitch rode alongside her.

Pointing she continued, "I found him right there. He had a chest wound. We ...uh... spoke for a few moments and he passed out. I screamed for help and then I woke up."

"Grant Anderson, hmmm... Do you know him?"

"No, I don't.

"Do you know what regiment he was with?"

"The third Kentucky," she answered, marveling that she could remember such a detail from her dream.

"Amazing!" he marveled.

"What?"

"You say you've never been here before?" he asked

"No"

"Has anyone ever told you about Snodgrass Hill or what happened here?"

"No, no one. Why?"

"Well, the Union regiments that fought here were primarily from Ohio, Indiana, and Pennsylvania, but the 3rd Kentucky fought here as well – exactly in the area that you're pointing to right now." Mitch couldn't deny the eerie shiver that ran up his arms and caused the hair on the back of his neck to stand on end.

"Really? How could I know this Mr. Garrison? Why would I dream this?" she muttered shaking her head.

"I have no idea," he shrugged his shoulders, still amazed by her detailed description. "Do you know anything about the cabin?"

"Like I said, there were horrifying screams coming from the direction of the house and two men carried wounded soldiers on stretchers to it," she answered.

"Let's go take a look and see if it jogs a memory," Mitch ascended the hill and dismounted his horse, tying him to a tree. Rebecca followed him cautiously. She wasn't sure she wanted to know what went on in the little cabin. But she nudged Midnight forward and dismounted, tying the horse to the tree next to Mitch's calico.

Mitch had already stepped toward the front door of the cabin which was no bigger than eleven by nine feet. The log cabin had three doors – one at the front, one on the left and another on the right. A window and chimney ran along the back wall. Mitch opened the creaky door and stepped inside, his boots scuffling along the wooden floorboards.

"Come on inside for a minute," he motioned.

Reluctantly she stepped into the house and glanced around, running her hand along the fireplace mantel, the back of a wooden chair and a small table. A wave of light-headness spread over her when...

Two men held down a Confederate soldier while a third carried a saw in his hand.

63

"We're out of ether," a wide-eyed union soldier gasped.

"No! You can't cut off my leg without anything!" the soldier screamed.

"We have to. You'll die if we don't," the doctor's sympathetic eyes glistened with moisture. "I'm so sorry son."

She flung her hands to her ears but nothing could deafen her to the horrible blood curdling screams. She leaned her head into Grant's shoulder as hot tears stung her eyes. At that moment she felt relieved that Grant's wound was in his chest. They couldn't cut that off. Within minutes the horrifying screams stifled and she lifted her head from Grant's shoulder and gazed into his eyes, "Grant, Grant! Talk to me Grant!" She squeezed his arm, but he didn't move. His steel blue eyes stared blankly at the ceiling with a slight smile on his face.

"Miss, he's gone," the dark-haired man who had helped carry Grant to the make-shift hospital knelt beside him and felt his pulse.

"No! He can't be dead. We're to be married!" she cried.

"I'm sorry Miss. He's gone," he patted her shoulder, but she pulled herself to her feet as two men came and lifted Grant's body from the stretcher.

"Where are you taking him?" she cried.

"We've very little space here and we need it for the living," one of the Confederate soldiers who held Grant's feet explained.

"I have my horse outside. I'll take him with me," she told them. She felt numb all over.

"I don't think that's wise, Miss."

"I don't care if you think it's wise. I'm not leavin' him here to be eaten by coyotes!" she demanded loudly.

Her outburst caught the Union physician's attention. "Make a note of him in the log book and let her take the body. We won't have time or means to give him a proper burial like she would anyway."

"Thank you, Sir! I'll go get my horse," she turned and fled sobbing from the little building.

"Miss Marchant, are you all right?" he asked. When Rebecca didn't answer, Mitch took her by the shoulders and stood in front of her.

"Miss Marchant, are you all right?"

She closed her eyes and shook her head, brushing at the tears that streamed from her eyes. "He died here," she whispered.

"Who?" her hushed tone caused him to whisper as well.

"Grant Anderson," she answered. "Oh, it was horrible! The amputations without anesthesia! The blood, the carnage!" she exclaimed. "The smell of it! It's nauseating!"

Mitch instinctively reached forward, brushing the tears from her cheeks. "It's ok," he soothed.

Without thinking she put her arms around his waist and buried her head in his shoulder. At first he stood motionless and made no effort to return her embrace.

"Why? Why do I keep seeing these things?" she pleaded.

He put his arms around her and comfortingly stroked her silky black hair, "Maybe you're tied to it somehow."

"How?" she looked up into his gray-blue eyes that gazed sympathetically into hers. "Did they really treat both sides here?" she asked incredulously.

"Yes, they did, remarkable isn't it?" he still couldn't believe she'd know such details without ever being told or visiting the location before. "Who is this Grant Anderson you keep speaking of?"

"I have no idea! But someone was in love with him and he intended to marry her," Rebecca shook her head and realized she still stood in Mitch's embrace. Suddenly coming to her senses, she released her grasp on him and stepped back shyly. "I'm sorry," she muttered.

"For what?"

"For ... for flinging myself at you," her embarrassed gaze dropped to the floor.

"Oh, well in such circumstances I'd imagine it would be understandable. I mean after seeing... Did you just see this scene while we've been standin' here?"

"Yes... you think I'm crazy, don't you?" she shook her head closing her eyes.

He stepped forward taking her by the shoulders, "No, I don't. Really I don't. How could you be crazy or imaginin' things when you know so many details that there's no other way you could know?"

"So you think what I'm seeing is real?" her eyes pleaded with him for she was uncertain of her own sanity.

"I think they must be echoes from the past or somethin'," he released his grip on her shoulders. "What else have you seen?"

Rebecca breathed deeply and exhaled. "I see men fighting in the fog. I see them killing each other at the creek, and having their arms and legs amputated in this horrific place. I see Grant dying here in her arms." She hesitated, "I see her alone with Grant on other occasions." She paused and then continued, "You know what's the oddest thing of all?"

"What?"

"I have no idea who *she* is because I'm always her. It's as if I'm reliving her memories! I feel what she feels! I see what she sees! Every wave of emotion from euphoria to guilt to pain, anguish, humiliation, love and horror – I feel all of it, Mr. Garrison!"

He wondered what she meant by euphoria and guilt, but something told him that perhaps now was not the time to ask. So he thought of another question, "You mentioned she was with him on other occasions. Do you know the locations of those meetings?"

"Well, actually it was just one other location besides here at Snodgrass Field and in this house. It was in the stable back at Soquili." She noted the perplexed expression on his face.

"So it does tie back to you!" a spark of illumination crossed his eyes.

"What do you mean?"

"Well, I mean it at least ties back to Soquili which ties to you. So they were in the stable together? Is that why you were lookin' around in there this morning?"

"Uh, yes," she blushed slightly and walked to the window.

"They had a rendezvous of sorts there," she mumbled.

"What do you mean?"

She didn't answer him.

"Are there others besides these two people in your dreams?" he pressed.

She turned to face him again and leaned against the window sill. "Of course there are the doctors and men carrying stretchers and thousands of dying soldiers on the ground... Wait..."

"What?" he asked anxiously taking a step toward her.

"There was someone in the stable with them. Someone who looked familiar to me." Mitch stood waiting for her to continue. She struggled to find a delicate way to relate the dream without violating all sense of propriety. "They were interrupted in the hayloft by a stocky man with straight, thinning black hair. His eyes seem familiar somehow, but I can't put my finger on where I've seen him before. He was angry at them for being alone in the loft and demanded that Grant marry her. His eyes were filled with hurt and rage. He seemed to know her very well. He scolded her and threw Grant out of the hayloft. She felt so much guilt and embarrassment!"

Rebecca stopped abruptly. Perhaps she'd said too much. She glanced timidly up at Mitch who stood motionless. He read between the lines what her words didn't say and he nervously kicked at a pebble at his feet.

"Did they ever get married?" he asked, looking up at her.

"No, he died before they could," she whispered, turned her back to him and stared out the window.

"So let's try to piece this together here," he suggested. "A Union soldier named Lieutenant Grant Anderson fell in love with a woman who lived at Soquili. Or do you think the Lieutenant lived there?"

"I'm not sure," she shook her head.

"Ok so one of them lived at Soquili and she evidently spent some intimate moments with the Lieutenant in the hayloft of the stable and as a result someone responsible for her found them and demanded that the Lieutenant do the right thing. Is that a fair assessment?" he asked.

"Yes, I'd say that's accurate," she stared at the floor and wondered why she felt guilty and embarrassed about someone else's sins.

"Evidently after that, Grant went off to battle here at Snodgrass Hill, was wounded and she came lookin' for him. He ended up dyin' in this very house in her arms before they were able to marry. That sound about right?" he asked.

"Yes, that's right," she nodded.

"Is there anything else?"

"Well, she took his body with her on the back of her horse. Or at least I know she planned to," Rebecca explained.

"Hmmm… I wonder where she buried him?" he mumbled.

She gulped, "Oh, I hadn't thought about that. Of course, before talkin' this through with you, I just thought I was dreamin' strange things. I didn't think about it being about real people! You truly think these are real people?"

"I don't know, but it certainly warrants some investigation, don't you think?" he asked.

"Yes, I suppose you're right. It just seems so silly to be researching a dream," she shook her head and rubbed her temples.

"It would be silly if your dreams weren't so accurate, but you've told me things there's no way you should know, Miss Marchant."

"Thank you, Mr. Garrison," she suddenly felt an immense gratitude for him.

"For what?" his eyebrows lowered.

"For believing me – for not thinking I'm crazy and for helping me make some sense of what's happening to me."

"You're welcome," he folded his arms across his broad chest.

"I'm sorry, but I need to get out of this house," she suddenly passed him and exited through the front door. Staring up into the blue sky she breathed deeply and exhaled. He came up behind her and although he didn't touch her, she could feel the warmth emanating from his body behind her.

"Are you all right?" he asked.

"Oh as well as anyone can be when she's walkin' around with a dead person's memories in her head!" she snapped.

"A dead person? What makes you think she's dead?" he asked.

She turned to face him, "Oh, I guess I don't know that do I? I have no reason to think she's dead. She could still be livin', couldn't she? After all, they fought this battle only eighteen years ago. There's no reason to think she's dead. She'd be in her late thirties, I'd guess by the age of the Lieutenant. Maybe I can find her and she can help me make sense of all this!"

"But you don't even know who she is," he reminded her.

"That's right," her shoulders slumped dejectedly.

"But we can start by lookin' for Grant Anderson," he smiled and lifted her chin with his finger. She felt the same fluttering in the pit of her stomach as she experienced in her dreams. She found herself feeling for Mitch what the girl in her dreams felt for Grant and it startled her. It was at that moment that she fully understood what her father meant by "sparks."

She stepped back from him nervously and suggested, "I guess we should be getting back before Grandma gets worried."

"Yeah, I guess you're right," he nodded and they untied their horses and started down the hill.

"Don't suppose you saw Old Green Eyes in any of your dreams?" he chuckled as they crossed the field.

"Who is this Old Green Eyes anyway? My uncle mentioned it, but wouldn't explain."

"So you haven't heard about our infamous ghost?"

"No... please tell me."

"It might give you nightmares," he warned.

She rolled her eyes, "As if I could have any worse than I'm already having!"

"Good point," he conceded. "Well, there's two theories on Old Green Eyes. First one is that he's a Confederate soldier who lost his head to a cannonball. They say they only found his head and now he's out searching for his body. But some say they saw him roaming among the dead here in Snodgrass Field the day of the battle and that he's more of a beast than a man. Supposedly, he has greenish-yellow eyes, long hair and fang-like teeth."

"Well, that just sounds silly," she chuckled and then realized that most people would find her ramblings infantile as well. "I guess I don't have a right to call anything silly though, do I?"

He chuckled and continued, "Some say he's from the Spanish American War when the men encamped and trained here on Snodgrass Hill. A lot of men died here from influenza. Others say that the Cherokees saw him even before that. Needless to say, no one wants to hang around Snodgrass Hill after dark."

"Do you believe he's real?" she studied him intently as he rode along beside her.

"Oh, I don't know. Does seem a bit far fetched. I think I'd find him more believable if they didn't make 'im out to be such a beast. I mean, I can believe in ghosts, but heinous, fanged ghostly beasts just don't strike me as believable."

"I see what you mean," she nodded.

As they rode along back toward the bridge, Rebecca noticed that she felt as if a weight had been lifted from her shoulders. Confiding in Mitch had freed her somehow. She began to see her visions and dreams more objectively. Having someone who believed her and wanted to help her get to the bottom of them comforted her.

They took the horses back to the stables, removed their saddles and bridles and dried the horses with towels. Rebecca couldn't help glancing over to Mitch as he patted the calico's back. "Would you like to come in for lunch?" she invited before she had thought through the forwardness of such a suggestion.

"Oh, I usually go home for lunch," he shrugged.

"Hilda's a great cook! She might still have some of that pumpkin pie from yesterday," she smiled.

"I don't know. Do you think your grandmother would want the hired help eatin' with the family?"

She hadn't thought of him feeling like hired help. "I have a feeling Grandma wouldn't mind."

"Why don't you ask her to be certain. I wouldn't want your Uncle Edmund getting upset with me," he suggested.

"I think Uncle Edmund is out of town, but I'll quickly go ask Grandma. Stay here and I'll be right back," she briskly approached the house and entered the front door. She went into the living room, "Grandma, you in here?" She wasn't there so she continued on to the kitchen, "Miss Hilda, is Grandma around?"

"She's upstairs in her sittin' room readin' a book I think," Hilda answered.

"That sure smells good! Any chance you have enough for one more body at lunch?"

"I should have plenty. Why?"

"I was thinking of asking Mr. Garrison to come in for lunch, but I need to ask Grandma first," she smiled.

"Oh, yes, you better ask your Grandma about that," the smile faded from the old woman's expression.

Rebecca didn't pay much attention to her, figuring Hilda was from the old school where servants didn't socialize with their employers. She exited the kitchen, went back to the entryway and scurried up the staircase. She strolled down the corridor and tapped lightly on her grandmother's bedroom door, "Grandma? May I come in?"

"Certainly, dear, come on in," Jemima greeted from the other side.

"Grandma, would you mind if I invited Mr. Garrison in for lunch?" she asked hopefully.

Jemima thought for a moment. "Yes, that would be delightful! Do that. Grumpy Edmund is out of town and it would be nice to have a handsome face to admire over lunch for a change," Jemima giggled.

"You are so funny, Grandma! Thank you!" Rebecca called over her shoulder as she left the room and hurried back downstairs and outside.

Crossing back to the stables, her heart fluttered as she saw him leaning his shoulder against the stable doorway with his foot crossed and propped up on the toe of his boot. *He is incredibly handsome* she thought to herself.

"Grandma said to come on in and join us for lunch. Uncle Edmund is out of town, so he won't be joining us today," she motioned for him to follow her. He caught up to her and as he took her arm lightly in his hand she caught her breath with the thrill his touch sent through her body. Her eyes glanced over at him questioningly.

"Does your Grandma know about your dreams? About the things you've been sensing and seeing?"

"No, and I'd really prefer she didn't if you don't mind. I think she'd think me a silly child with a wild imagination," Rebecca explained.

"All right. I just didn't want to put my foot in anythin'," he winked and let go of her arm. He quickened his pace so that he passed her slightly and held the front door open for her.

As Mitch and Rebecca entered the house, Jemima descended the stairs. "Thank you for joining us, Mr. Garrison!" she greeted jovially.

"Thank you for invitin' me, Ma'am," he pulled his hat from his head and placed it on a rack by the door.

Jemima pointed to the right, "There's a wash room through there if you'd like to clean up before lunch."

"Ladies first," he extended his hand in the direction of the washroom. Rebecca went into the small room with a wash basin and shut the door behind her.

"So, did you two have a nice ride?" Jemima looked up into Mitch's face. He stood a full foot taller than her five-foot four-inch frame.

"Yes, it's perfect weather out. Not too hot, not too cold," he nodded.

"I really do appreciate you takin' the time to show my granddaughter around. She could use the company of someone more her age."

"My pleasure, Ma'am," he nodded.

Rebecca opened the door and he passed her and disappeared behind the door.

"Grandma, why do you have that possum grin on your face?" Rebecca just knew that her grandmother must have been giving Mitch a hard time.

"Nothin', dear, nothin' at all. I don't even know what you mean," she defended.

"You said somethin' embarrassin' to him, didn't you?" she asked.

"Honey, I would never do somethin' like that to you. We were just talkin' about the weather," she smiled innocently.

Rebecca shook her finger at her grandmother. "That better be all you were talkin' about," she scolded in a whisper and then chuckled wondering why she, a seventeen-year-old, felt the need to treat a sixty-three-year-old woman like a child.

The door to the washroom opened and Jemima motioned, "Let's go see what delicious ambrosia Hilda has for us today."

Mitch pulled out their chairs and seated himself across from Rebecca. They engaged in light conversation throughout lunch and then Rebecca turned to her grandmother, "Grandma, Grandpa Edmund died before I was born – right?"

"Yes, he died in the war," Jemima's eyes wrinkled quizzically. "Why dear?"

"Well, I never got to know him and I was wondering if there were any pictures around here of him?" Rebecca glanced at Mitch for a second and he gave her a knowing look. He knew where she was heading.

"There's a picture of him in your Uncle Edmund's study, dear," Jemima answered.

"Could I please see it? I'd love to know what he looked like," Rebecca asked.

"Certainly, dear. We'll go see if Edmund's left his study unlocked."

Rebecca anxiously rose to her feet. Mitch reached over and helped Jemima pull out her chair and Jemima led them to Edmund's study.

"We're in luck, Edmund left it unlocked today," she slowly opened the creaking oak door and the pungent odor of cigars wafted from the room.

"Excuse the smell. It's the only room I let Edmund smoke those stinky cigars in," Jemima explained as she crossed to a table and lit a lamp.

"There's my Ed," Jemima pointed to a portrait on the wall over Edmund's desk. A handsome brown-haired Confederate soldier who appeared to be in his mid-forties reminded Rebecca of her father.

"He looks like Papa more so than Uncle Edmund, don't you think, Grandma?" Rebecca observed.

"Yes, he does. Edmund looks more like your Grandpa's father whereas my Ed and Ethan looked like Ed's mother. She was a beautiful woman," Jemima explained.

"Do you have any more pictures of family members?" Rebecca asked.

"Well, let's see here," Jemima crossed the room to a wall covered with books. She pointed to a shelf over her head, "Mr. Garrison, could you reach up there and pull down that photograph box?"

"Yes, Ma'am," he reached up and retrieved an ornate wooden picture box and handed it to her.

She walked over to Edmund's desk, blew the dust from the top of the box and set it down on the desk. Carefully removing the lid, she picked up a few tin types from inside.

"This is your father and Edmund as boys," she handed the tin type to Rebecca.

Rebecca held the photograph so that Mitch could see it too, "Oh, weren't they cute!"

Mitch smiled and nodded.

"And here's one of me and your Grandpa on our wedding day," Jemima handed Rebecca a larger photograph.

"Oh, Grandma! You were beautiful! And Grandpa was so handsome!"

"You look a bit like your grandmother there, Miss Marchant," Mitch observed.

"Yes, I think so too. We have the same eyes and high cheekbones and of course the dark hair," Jemima agreed.

"And here's one of your parents on their wedding day," Jemima handed the photograph to Rebecca and received the others she held out to her.

"These are just priceless!" Rebecca exuded excitedly. Mitch observed her quietly, noting how radiant she appeared when she smiled happily.

"And here is Uncle Edmund in his Confederate uniform. This was taken just before you were born," Jemima handed the picture to Rebecca whose mouth dropped open. Her hands began to tremble and her face grew pale.

Jemima still rummaged through the box, but Mitch noticed Rebecca's startled expression and put his hand to her back. Not wanting to draw attention to the obvious distress that Rebecca found in looking at her Uncle Edmund's photograph, Mitch moved between Rebecca and her grandmother and diverted the woman's attention, "This is just wonderful that you've kept all these pictures, Mrs. Marchant. My mother keeps our family's pictures too and I always loved rummaging through them as a boy. I know they mean a lot to you."

Mitch's diversion gave Rebecca time to collect herself. She set the photograph on the desk and rubbed her face in an effort to restore some color to what she felt certain were ghostly pale cheeks.

"Oh yes, Grandma, it's just wonderful that you've kept these! Do you have any more?" Rebecca put on her best effort to act enthusiastic.

Mitch glanced over his shoulder and realizing that Rebecca had collected herself. He stepped away from Jemima and made room for Rebecca to see the box of pictures.

Jemima flipped through the photographs in the box and Rebecca caught Mitch's eye, "Thank you!" she mouthed silently. He winked at her and turned back toward Jemima.

"Just these two left that you haven't seen," Jemima quickly put the photos back in the box and handed the remaining two to Rebecca. "This is you as a baby and this one is your Grandpa on his favorite horse."

"It looks like Midnight," Rebecca smiled.

"Yes, your Midnight is a descendant of Grandpa's Midnight," she explained.

"Oh, that makes me feel connected to him!" Rebecca smiled.

Jemima put out her hand to receive the photos, slipped them into the box and replaced the lid. Handing the box to Mitch she requested, "Mr. Garrison, could you please put this box back in its place?"

"Yes Ma'am," he took the box and replaced it on the upper shelf.

"Thank you, Grandma! I so enjoyed that!" Rebecca smiled, giving her grandmother a hug.

"You're welcome, dear," she squeezed Rebecca's hand. "Now if you don't mind, it's time for my afternoon nap." She walked back to the door and the pair followed her. She closed

the door behind them and they went back to the foyer.
"Thank you again for joining us for lunch, Mr. Garrison."

"Thank you, Ma'am!" he nodded and Rebecca and Mitch watched her ascend the staircase to retire to her room.

"What was that about in there?" he whispered once Jemima was gone.

Rebecca motioned for him to follow her out the front door. Without saying a word, she stepped off the porch and walked out to a corral and leaned her elbows on the fence.

"It was your Uncle Edmund's picture. What startled you about it?" he finally asked when she stood silently for a minute. She turned to face him, leaning one elbow on the fence.

"Uncle Edmund is the man who caught them in the stable," she whispered.

"Really?" his eyes widened.

"Yes, it's him. That's why he looked so familiar in the dream. His eyes are the same, but he never shows that much emotion in them and he's put on so much weight and lost so much hair that he doesn't look the same anymore. You saw the picture – right?"

"I caught a glimpse of it, yes. He does look quite different. Not sure I would have recognized it as him myself." He scratched his head, "So, that gives us another clue, doesn't it?"

"Yes it does! That means that the girl in the dream lived here at Soquili and that Uncle Edmund was responsible for her in some way."

"Maybe she was a servant here? A slave?" Mitch's eyes widened with possibility. "What if Grant Anderson was in love with a Negro slave?"

"Hmmm… may be! Maybe that *is* the mystery of it all!" Rebecca hoped they were on the right track because she wanted the disturbing dreams and visions to stop.

"So let's see if this makes sense then. Grant Anderson, a Lieutenant in the Union army, falls in love with a slave or servant girl here at Soquili. He compromises her virtue, your uncle Edmund catches them and insists that Anderson marry her. They plan to marry, but he's sent off to Snodgrass Hill where she finds him, gets him to the field hospital. He dies there in her arms and they let her take the body back with her."

"That's right," Rebecca nodded. "Do you think they'd let a slave take a Union officer's body with her?" Rebecca's eyes wrinkled with doubt.

"Hmmm… don't know about that. You wouldn't think so, would you?"

"Maybe she wasn't a slave. Maybe she was a white servant girl," Rebecca suggested.

"Oh! Why didn't I think of this before?" he slapped his thigh.

"What?"

"My family's lived next to the Soquili for years. I bet my mother would know if there was a white servant girl that worked here or if a slave girl fell in love with a Union officer." He nodded, "She just might know somethin'!"

"Will you ask her for me?" Rebecca looked up into his eyes.

"I will. But she's visiting my Aunt Mable in Athens and won't be back for another two weeks," he punched his fist into his hand in aggravation.

"Is there anyone else at your house who would know?"

"No, my Pa died a year ago and we haven't had servants since before the war."

"But, we have at least three or four servants here who lived through the war! If anyone would know about a servant or slave falling in love with a Union officer, a servant would!" Rebecca's eyes lit up excitedly.

"That's right!" his excited expression turned a bit more somber, "But how're you gonna approach 'em about it? If this is a Soquili scandal, they might not be willin' to talk about it. No one at Soquili may be willin' to talk about it."

"Hmmm... I hadn't considered that." She leaned both elbows on the fence and rubbed her temples with her hands.

"Maybe just stay with the obvious things you'd want to know about the family. I mean, a typical granddaughter who has never been to the home of her father's childhood has certain questions – just like you had today about the photographs. Maybe you could proceed under that guise and no one would expect that you were probing for skeletons in the closet," he suggested.

"Is that what I'm doing, Mr. Garrison?" she chuckled. "Probing for family skeletons?"

"Well, where there's ghosts there's skeletons," he teased. "And please stop callin' me Mr. Garrison. I think we know too many of each other's secrets for you to keep calling me that. Please, call me Mitch."

"Wait a minute," she held up her hand. "You know all *my* secrets. I don't know a single one of yours!" she teased. "Tell me at least one of *your* secrets and *then* we can move to a first name basis."

Mitch scratched his blonde head. "Hmmm… secrets about me? I'm just a borin' old horse trainer. Not got anythin' near as excitin' and mysterious as you with your hauntin' dreams and visions!" he winked.

"No secrets, no first names," she shook her head resolutely.

He thought for a moment. "Ok, here's one… My Pa had a brother who fought for the Union and of course I told you that my Pa was Confederate. Anyway, both of them ended up fightin' here at Chickamauga. It was in the skirmish at Jay's Mill. They came face to face with one another. Now mind you, these two fought like cats and dogs growin' up and my Pa was madder than a hornet when his brother Frank went off and fought with the Union. So here these two brothers are face to face in the woods over by Jay's Mill. They pointed their rifles at one another, cocked 'em and then my Pa went right and Uncle Frank went left and neither one of 'em looked back, just kept on walkin' as if they hadn't even seen one another."

"Did they ever reconcile?" Rebecca wondered.

"No, Frank met up with a bunch of Confederates hidin' in the underbrush – probably not even fifteen minutes later. Pa found 'im among the dead and knelt down next to 'im and cried like a baby. Pa said that's the only time he'd ever cried since he was a grown man. Never cried like that before nor since."

"How pitiful!" Rebecca's sad eyes glistened with moisture and Mitch thought that their dark brown tint turned a shade lighter.

"It is pitiful, isn't it?" he nodded. "We're lucky not to have experienced what our fathers went through."

"Yes we are!" she agreed.

"So will you call me Mitch now?" he grinned.

"I guess, although that wasn't really a secret about *you*," she pointed out.

"I don't think I've got any secrets." He leaned his elbow on the fence and thought for a moment. "Wait! I've got it!"

"What?" she asked expectantly.

"One time when I was just a stable boy over here at Soquili, I found one of your uncle Edmund's half-smoked cigars on the ground."

"Oh, don't tell me you smoked that stinky used thing!" she grimaced. She could just see one of Uncle Edmund's soppy gnawed-on cigars lying in the dirt.

"Yep, I carried it off to the creek, lit it up and smoked it. I thought I was goin' to throw up. I felt so green that I hid in the hayloft, curled up in a ball for a couple hours tryin' to recover," he chuckled, his pale blue eyes twinkling in the sunlight. "Good enough?"

"Yeah, I guess we have a deal then," she held out her hand to shake his on the agreement. He surprised her by taking her hand in his, lifting it to his lips and kissing it instead of the firm, friendly handshake she expected.

"Well, Rebecca, I must be gettin' to work. I've been too much a man o' leisure today and I've got three students this afternoon."

"Oh, I hope I haven't kept you from anything important," she apologized.

"Nothin' more important than helpin' you solve this mystery, Rebecca," he winked. She knew he just used her name repetitively to unsettle her. Or maybe he didn't realize what he was doing but what unnerved her even more than him calling her Rebecca was the fact that he still held her hand tenderly in his as he did so.

"I appreciate your help, Mitch," she wondered if the sound of his name on her lips made him as nervous as it did her. She could hardly believe she'd agreed to address him by his first name. It took her two months and a marriage proposal before she'd agreed to call Stephen by his first name. "Enjoy your work," she smiled and he finally released her hand. He leaned his back and elbows on the fence, grinning as his eyes followed her tall, slender form back to the house.

Stephen Rebecca thought to herself. It was the first time since arriving at Soquili that she'd even thought of her friend. She felt ashamed at herself that her attention could be so easily turned by a handsome face.

Chapter 4

*R*ebecca awoke refreshed the third morning after arriving at Soquili and breathed a sigh of relief that she had no disquieting dreams that night. She rose from her bed and looked out the window. A heavy thunderstorm poured outside, and she felt a bit disappointed that she wouldn't be able to spend time outside with Mitch. Most likely he'd only feed the horses and return home since he wouldn't be able to break any horses or train any students in this downpour. She dressed and descended the stairs for breakfast.

"Your Grandma won't be joinin' you for breakfast this mornin', Miss," Hilda informed her as she entered the kitchen.

"Why not?" Rebecca asked.

"She's feelin' poorly this mornin' and I carried her breakfast up to her room," Hilda explained.

"Is she all right? Maybe I should go check on her," Rebecca worriedly suggested.

"You're welcome to check on her, but she's just got a cold. She likes to get plenty o' rest when she gets a cold so that it doesn't turn into anythin' worse," Hilda explained. "Why don't you eat your breakfast and then join her?"

"All right, do you mind if I just stay in here in the kitchen and chat with you while I eat?" Rebecca asked.

"Not at all, Miss. I'd enjoy the company," Hilda smiled.

Rebecca retrieved a plate from the cabinet and helped herself to the eggs, bacon and biscuits. She sat down at a little round table in the kitchen and motioned for Hilda to join her. The elderly woman sat next to her and they ate together in silence for several minutes. Then Rebecca decided she'd take this opportunity to learn what she could about the history of the property.

"I've really enjoyed learnin' about the battlefield and the history of Soquili since I've been here. You were here even before the war, weren't you, Miss Hilda?" Rebecca began.

"Yes Miss, I've been here for nearly thirty-five years. Why, your uncle Edmund and your father were just young boys when I came," she smiled.

"Was Uncle Edmund so solemn even then?" Rebecca asked.

"Oh, no, Miss. He ran and played and laughed. He was quite a prankster as a child, if I remember correctly," Hilda confided.

"Really?" Rebecca asked in surprise.

"Oh yes, he used to tease the other children mercilessly," she smiled.

"Other children? Were there other children at Soquili besides Uncle Edmund and my Papa?" Rebecca asked anxiously.

"Um… ya know the servants had children of course," Hilda twiddled her fork on her plate.

"Were they all boys or were there any girls?" Rebecca asked.

"There may have been a few girls among the lot," Hilda nodded.

Rebecca wished she knew something more about the girl from her dream so that she would know what to ask Hilda next. "Was Uncle Edmund good friends with any of them?"

"Not that I recall," Hilda shook her head. "He just teased 'em all about equal I'd say."

"Did he ever have a girlfriend?" Rebecca asked.

"He went out with girls, but he didn't ever officially court anyone that I can remember." Hilda shrugged her shoulders and scooped some food onto her fork.

Rebecca started to feel frustrated that her line of questioning was getting her nowhere. So she decided to play the only card she had, "Have you ever heard of a Union soldier named Grant Anderson?"

Hilda stopped her fork mid-air before it reached her mouth, "Umm… what was that name again?"

"Lieutenant Grant Anderson. He was a Union soldier that I think may have courted a girl here at Soquili," she figured if she was going to play the card, she may as well let Hilda examine it fully.

Hilda put the fork of food in her mouth and chewed in silence, her eyes rolling up into her head as if she were trying to remember something. Rebecca continued to watch the woman expectantly.

"Grant Anderson... Grant Anderson... I don't recall," Hilda shook her head. "Where'd ya hear o' 'im?"

"Oh," Rebecca hadn't thought about Hilda asking her where she got her information. She finally decided to shift the blame to someone who couldn't deny it, "My mother mentioned somethin' to me one time about a Lieutenant Grant Anderson courtin' a young woman at Soquili. She just mentioned what a handsome man he was... we were talkin' about handsome men at the time..."

"Oh, so your mother told you about this Lieutenant Anderson?" Hilda asked. "Did she tell you anythin' else about 'im? It's been so long ago maybe if you told me a bit more I would remember 'im."

Relieved that Hilda bought her story she ventured on, "Well, let's see. He had thick wavy brown hair and amazing steel blue eyes, very muscular, tall and he died in the Battle of Chickamauga on Snodgrass Hill before he could marry the girl he loved. Was quite a tragic tale – I believe we were reading *Romeo and Juliet* at the time and so the combination of that tragic tale and our discussion of handsome men brought mother around to the story." Rebecca had never told such a string of lies in her life, but if it would help her glean more information from Hilda, then so be it.

"Hmm... doesn't ring a bell. Who was the girl?" Hilda asked.

"I don't know. Mother didn't say. I only know that she was crushed when her officer died and that she found him there at the battlefield and begged the Union officers to let her take his body home with her," Rebecca replied.

"Hmm…" Hilda rubbed her chin, thinking pensively. Hilda rose from her seat and put her plate in a pail of sudsy water.

"So do you remember the girl, Miss Hilda?" Rebecca pressed.

"Hmm… I don't recall anythin' like that ever happenin' 'round here," Hilda shook her head.

Rebecca rose from her seat and put her dishes on the counter by Hilda. She felt certain Hilda was hiding something.

"Why don't you run along and check on your Grandma, Miss?" Hilda suggested.

As Rebecca left the kitchen she realized that she'd laid a lot on the table for Hilda and gotten nothing in return. Buried in her thoughts, she climbed the staircase and reached her grandmother's room. She tapped lightly on the door.

"Yes?" Jemima's stuffy voice answered from the other side.

"I'm sorry to bother you, Grandma. I just wanted to check on you and see if I could get you anything. May I come in?" Rebecca answered.

"Come on in dear," Jemima welcomed her.

Rebecca opened the door slowly and entered her grandmother's room. It was decorated in burgundy bedding and drapes and a low fire burned in the fireplace.

"Oh, Grandma, you poor thing! You don't look like you feel very well at all!" Rebecca noted.

"I'm well enough. I just have a stuffy nose and a sore throat," Jemima pushed her pillow so that it would prop her upright.

"Oh, please don't sit up on my account," Rebecca held up her hand indicating that Jemima should sit still. "Can I get anything for you? Would you like me to put another log on the fire or bring you a drink?"

"You could put another log on. This fall weather can't make up its mind if it wants to be hot or cold and with this thunderstorm, there's a bit of a chill in the air," Jemima answered.

Rebecca went to the fire and placed another log on the embers. "Can I get you anything else?"

"No thank you, dear. Hilda's keepin' me well fed and brought this pitcher of hot sassafras tea for me. Feels good on my throat," she smiled weakly. "Make yourself at home now, I know you love bein' outside and I hate that you're stuck in here all day! You know where the cross-stitch is and Uncle Edmund has lots of books in his study."

"Thank you, Grandma, but you don't need to be concerned about me. I can entertain myself," Rebecca smiled. "If you don't need anything else, I'll leave you to rest."

"Thank you, dear," Jemima watched as Rebecca left the room and shut the door behind her.

Rebecca didn't feel like sewing or reading, so she decided to take her grandmother's advice and make herself at home. She'd use this time to explore the big old house. Perhaps she'd turn up some clues.

Hilda knocked lightly on Jemima's door, "Ma'am, may I come in for a moment?"

"Yes," Jemima answered.

Hilda entered the room carrying a bowl of peppermint candies and shut the door behind her, "I thought these might help your throat, Ma'am."

"How thoughtful of you, Hilda! You're always so good to me," Jemima smiled and took one of the candies from the bowl and put it in her mouth.

Hilda placed the bowl on the night table as she sat down in the chair next to Jemima's bed, "Ma'am, I hate to bother you when you have a cold, but there's somethin' rather important I need to talk with you about."

The nervous expression on Hilda's face made Jemima uneasy and she sat upright in her bed, propping herself up on her stack of pillows. Hilda reached forward and helped her adjust them.

"What is it Hilda? You look as if you've seen a ghost!"

"Well, you ain't too far off Ma'am," Hilda wrung her hands nervously as Jemima's eyes fixed on her. "Ma'am, Miss Rebecca wanted me to join her for breakfast in the kitchen this mornin'. So we sat down and ate and she began to ask me about her uncle Edmund as a boy and about the other children at Soquili and if there were any girls here."

"She did?" Jemima's eyes widened. "What did you tell her?"

"She caught me off guard, Ma'am. I told her that of course the servants had youngins and some of 'em was girls." Jemima nodded satisfied with her servant's explanation. "Then, plum out o' the blue, she asked me if I ever heard of a ..." Hilda's voice lowered to a soft whisper, "Lieutenant Grant Anderson!"

"What?" Jemima leaned forward and she just about choked on her peppermint as one of her pillows fell to the floor. Hilda picked up the pillow and placed it back behind Jemima. "What did you tell her?" she coughed.

"Well, I pretended I didn't remember and I turned it around and asked her how she knew of 'im. And she said that her Mama told her about 'im – said they was readin' *Romeo and Juliet* together and talkin' about handsome men and tragic love stories and that her Mama told her that Lieutenant Anderson was a handsome man and that he fell in love with a girl here at Soquili, but that he died over on Snodgrass Hill before they had a chance to marry."

"She knew all o' that?" Jemima's mouth dropped.

"She described 'im to the letter, Ma'am. That's what was amazin' to me. It was almost like she'd seen 'im herself," Hilda's eyes widened.

"She did?" Jemima scratched her head. "You didn't tell her anythin' did you?"

"Oh, no Ma'am! You gave me strict instructions! I just let her do the talkin'" Hilda shook her head nervously. "But I thought you'd want to know ma'am."

"I wonder why Caroline and Ethan would make such a fuss about Rebecca never knowing about all this and then Caroline goes and tells her about Grant. Doesn't make any sense, does it?" Jemima scratched her head.

"No ma'am, it doesn't," Hilda rose from the chair. "Do you need anythin' before I go, Ma'am?"

"No, I'm fine. Thank you, Hilda, for handlin' that so well and lettin' me know."

"Yes'm," Hilda left the room and shut the door behind her. Jemima flopped back on her pillow and rubbed her temples. The last thing she wanted weighing on her mind while she was sick was worries about Rebecca's questions regarding Grant Anderson and ...

Rebecca wandered through the corridors of the large plantation house, jiggling doorknobs and looking in the empty rooms. Finally she ended up in front of Edmund's study, turned the doorknob and opened it slowly. The gray dreary day made it difficult to see, so Rebecca lit the lamp and adjusted the wick. She looked around the room, standing in front of his big oak desk scattered with papers. She began to grow light-headed and suddenly a much younger Edmund sat before her.

"I don't want you seein' him anymore," Edmund's dark brown eyes squinted with anger as he sat behind his desk.

"Why? Why can't I see 'im anymore?" she could feel her anger rising within her.

"He's a traitor – headin' off to join the Union! No decent Southerner would even consider such a thing!" he raged.

"But he feels very strongly that everyone should be free – no matter their color," she hoped she could help Edmund understand Grant's side of the situation. "Surely with your Cherokee heritage you can understand the plight of those who are persecuted because of their race!"

"This war's about a lot more than slavery, girl! It's about state's rights. If we let the federal government become all-powerful, 'fore we know it they'll be meddlin' in all our affairs and every last one of us'll be slaves! The states must remain sovereign or soon we'll lose all our freedoms. There's other ways to deal with the slavery issue than destroyin' states rights in the process." Edmund vehemently argued his point.

"Maybe if you'd stay calm and try to explain that to 'im, he'd see what you mean. But when you start yellin' and flyin' into a rage, it just makes 'im dig in his heels and think you're crazy," she argued.

"I've tried talkin' with 'im calmly about it, but it doesn't do a lick o' good. That boy's as thick headed and stubborn as a mule!" Edmund leaned his elbows on his desk, rubbing his temples.

"And you're not?" it slipped off her tongue before she could retract it.

"Enough o' that! I've given you an order and I expect you to obey it. You won't be seein' Grant Anderson again."

"I'm not one of your soldiers, Edmund! You can't bark orders at me and expect me to…"

"You'll do what I say. I'm in charge here at Soquili now and you'll do as you're told."

"You're not the final say 'round here and you know it! And I'm old enough to decide who I want to keep company with!" She turned and stormed out of the room, slamming his study door behind her.

Rebecca shook her head as she returned from her reverie. She went to the window to see if it was still raining. She needed to talk this over with Mitch. But the rain still poured outside and she knew he wouldn't be around. She decided to get her mind off of it all instead and scanned Edmund's bookshelf for a light-hearted book to divert her attention, she reached up and pulled a book from the shelf, left the study and went upstairs to lie down in her bed and read for a while.

Rebecca read for several hours until her eyes grew heavy and she could no longer keep them open. Finally, she leaned her head back on her pillow and drifted off to sleep.

She scurried off into the woods to where she had tied the stallion to a tree. Fortunately she had hidden him well, for he still waited there for her return. She untied the animal and rode back at full speed toward Snodgrass Hill to retrieve the body of her beloved. She dismounted the horse upon reaching the entrance of the cabin, holding the reins securely in her hands.

"I've brought my horse, please help me put Lieutenant Anderson's body upon his back," she asked the Union soldier who had helped her earlier. He and another man came forward carrying the Lieutenant's body and flung it over the back of the horse. She pulled some rope from her saddle bag and tenderly, but securely fastened the body in place atop the horse.

"Thank you, Sir, for your help," she told the Union soldier.

"Be careful, Miss. A fine horse like that is sure to draw attention. I'm amazed you got this far without someone stealin' it from you," he warned.

She reached over and pulled up the pant leg of her Lieutenant and removed a pistol strapped to his calf. "Thank you. I can take care of myself well enough." Holding the pistol in her hand, she left the hill on foot, leading the stallion by the reins.

Having some idea where soldiers lurked, she took a wooded route home, to avoid possible assailants from either side. As she approached Soquili, her heart sank to see the main stable nothing more than a smoldering mound, its yellow and orange embers burning in the last moments before darkness completely enveloped the sky. The plantation house windows lay in shattered glass along the ground. But the house still stood, which was more than she could say for other homes she had passed in her travels. Most were burned completely to the ground, leaving nothing but a chimney standing where fine homes once graced the landscape. For some unknown reason or divine act of Providence, Soquili had been spared from the incendiaries.

Peering around to make sure no one lay in wait in the shadows, she carefully approached the house, still leading the stallion with Grant's body on its back. As she reached the door, she tied the stallion to a front porch column and stepped up toward the door. With the door securely bolted from inside and all the windows boarded shut, she could not enter, so she began to pound on the door.

"Please, let me in! Can you hear me?"

"Who is it?" came a voice from inside.

"It's me, Sabrina!"

She could hear the wrenching of boards being pulled from the door and after a minute, the door opened and Jemima flung her arms around her, "My goodness, dear! We thought we'd lost you? Wherever have you been?"

"I went for Grant," she brushed the tears from her eyes.

Jemima flung both her hands to her mouth, "Oh dear! Is he? Is he..?"

"Yes, Ma'am. He's dead. I begged them to let me take the body so he wouldn't be eaten by coyotes," she explained through her broken sobs.

"Jefferson, please help us get Lieutenant Anderson's body indoors!" Jemima called.

Jefferson scurried from the house and Sabrina and Jefferson untied the body and carried it into the house. "And get the horse inside as well. We can't leave him out there. They've stole all but two mares and this stallion," Jemima instructed.

"You want the horse inside the house?" she gasped.

"If we're ever to rebuild Soquili, we need these horses. He's the only stud we have. Bring him on in the great room."

"Yes, Ma'am," she pulled the stallion's reins, tugging him up the porch steps and through the door.

"Jefferson, Hilda, let's get this boarded back up before they return!" Jemima grabbed a hammer and helped Jefferson and Hilda hammer the boards back in place. The hammering became louder and louder until Rebecca woke and sat up in her bed. Someone knocked solidly at her door.

"Miss Rebecca?" Hilda called from the other side of the door. "Dinner's ready Miss Rebecca. Are you in there?"

Rebecca rose from her bed and unlocked the door. Hilda stood on the other side.

"Are you all right Miss? You never came down for lunch and it's already dinner time," Hilda's face held genuine concern.

"I'm all right. I just got to readin' and then fell asleep. Let me wash up and I'll be right down."

"Yes Miss," Hilda left and Rebecca closed the door.

Rebecca splashed water on her face and looked at herself in the mirror, "Sabrina! I know her name now! It's Sabrina!" she whispered aloud as she suddenly remembered the dream. Unsure of what to do with this new information, she dried her hands and face with a towel and descended the stairs for dinner, determined to investigate the name on her own instead of asking Hilda anything further. Hilda's hesitance and guilty expressions when asked about Grant betrayed her knowledge of more than she would tell and Rebecca assumed that the servant was simply obeying orders with her silence. Rebecca decided that it wasn't safe to ask Edmund or Jemima anything further. Mitch would be her only confident and speaking to him would have to wait until morning.

Jemima ate in her bedroom that evening, so when Rebecca entered the dining room, she found that her uncle Edmund had returned and sat at the head of the table.

"Good evening, Uncle Edmund," Rebecca smiled.

"Good evening, Rebecca," Edmund nodded. As she reached the table, he rose from his chair and pulled hers out for her. Once she had seated herself, he returned to his seat and they both waited in silence for Hilda to bring the food to the table.

"Did you have a good trip, Uncle?" Rebecca tried to make pleasant conversation although her Uncle made her uneasy – especially since the majority of her encounters with him were intensely emotional ones from her reveries. Matter of fact, Rebecca knew more about Edmund of the past than she did Edmund of the present.

"Yes, it was a profitable trip. Sold four thoroughbreds for a tidy sum," Edmund looked toward the kitchen door as Hilda entered with two steaming plates of food.

"Thank you!" Rebecca smiled at Hilda as she set the plate before her.

"You're welcome, Miss," Hilda responded and went back into the kitchen.

"Uncle, I've been thinking about something and I was wondering if I might ask you a few questions about the war," Rebecca decided there were some things she could ask her uncle that could help her piece together a picture of Soquili during the last days of the Civil War and immediately following.

"Really?" Edmund's eyebrows rose, "Not too many young women care a thing for war."

"I like history," Rebecca smiled. "And it seems we're living in the middle of it."

"That we are," Edmund nodded, "Ask away." He put a bite of pot roast in his mouth and looked at her inquisitively.

Rebecca fancied that her uncle Edmund actually might be pleased to join in this conversation so she began encouraged, "So many of the homes were destroyed during the war. How did Soquili survive? I mean, what kind of damage was done and how did you keep the horse farm running? Weren't horses a prime mark for theft?"

Edmund nodded, impressed by his niece's thoughtful question, "You're right. They burned most of the houses 'round here to the ground. How Soquili escaped is truly a miracle I suppose. We're really not sure why they didn't burn the house, but they did burn the main stable and drove all the horses from it. They stole all but three of the horses."

"How were you able to save the three?" Rebecca asked and then scooped up a fork of mashed potatoes.

"Two of our best mares were grazing on the back part of the property. Your grandmother went out herself and brought them into the house and hid them in there in the great room. The only stallion we had left to start the farm over with was Midnight. We think their hands were so full roundin' up the horses that they didn't bother with the house. Your grandmother, Ol' Jefferson and Hilda boarded the animals up inside the house until the battle was over.

"Was that Grandfather's Midnight?" Rebecca asked.

"No, it was actually the son of Father's Midnight," Edmund explained.

"We have Midnight Silhouette that we entered in the Derby this year – is he a descendant of Grandpa's Midnight?"

"He is. Your Papa took the brother of the Midnight that was spared during the war and started his farm in Kentucky with him. Your Papa had him with him in the war."

"So how was Soquili's Midnight spared during the war?"

"Uh, someone was out ridin' him when the Union soldiers stole the horses and brought him back after they'd left."

"Oh really? Who had him?" Rebecca tried to act nonchalant with that question.

"Can't remember, I really wasn't here at the time," Edmund put another fork of food in his mouth and chewed it busily.

"So you rebuilt everything with those three horses then?"

"Uh hum," Edmund nodded still chewing his food. "You better finish up your dinner before it gets cold," Edmund pointed to Rebecca's plate which had hardly been touched because she'd been so busily asking him questions.

"Oh," she glanced down at her plate, "I guess I should."

The remainder of their meal was eaten in silence. When Edmund had finished his last bite, he rose from his seat, flung his napkin into his chair and rubbed his protruding belly. "I'll be in my study if anyone needs me."

"Good night, Uncle," Rebecca told him as he passed her.

"Good night," he nodded and left the room.

The next morning was as damp and gray as the one before. Rebecca stood at the window as rain drizzled down. She looked toward the stable and saw Mitch entering to feed the horses. Raining or not, Rebecca decided that she must speak to him. She had too much new information to share and discuss. She quickly dressed and crept down the stairs. It was early and Hilda still hadn't prepared breakfast.

102

Rebecca threw her shawl over her head, slipped out the back terrace off the great room and lifted her dress as she ran to the barn.

"Whatcha doin' out in this muck this mornin' Rebecca?" Mitch smiled, lifting his gaze from the oats he poured into Midnight's trough.

"I've got some new information," she breathed heavily as she pulled the wet shawl from around her head, wrung the water from it and laid it across a railing.

"Oh really?" he set down the feed sack and leaned his elbow on the stall. His appearance distracted her. He was drenched from head to toe and his shirt clung to his muscular torso.

"Uh – let's see.. where to begin?" she stammered.

"Start with the beginnin'," he grinned. "What did you learn first?"

"Why don't I start with what I didn't learn," she smiled. "First of all, Hilda's hidin' somethin'. I asked her about the other young people who lived at Soquili and she said there were girls here, but when I asked her specifically about Grant Anderson, she stammered and then acted like she'd never heard of him."

"You asked her about Grant Anderson?" Mitch's eyebrows rose in surprise that Rebecca would be so bold.

"I was gettin' nowhere with her, so I figured I'd just be blunt and ask in hopes she'd give me a clue. But she claimed ignorance. I think she's lyin'." Rebecca's eyes squinted. "I just don't know why."

"So what else didn't you learn?" Mitch chuckled.

"Well, I'll just move on to what I *did* learn. I had a couple more visions or dreams or whatever these things are. One in Uncle Edmund's study and one was a dream about - Oh! Wait a minute the most important thing of all!" Rebecca's eyes grew wide.

"What?" Mitch chuckled at her animation.

"I know her name now! It's Sabrina."

"Sabrina? Hmm... Sabrina... that rings familiar somehow," Mitch scratched his head pensively.

"It does? Who is she? Where have you heard of her?" Rebecca fired questions at him.

"Slow down, let me think. Sabrina. I can't put my finger on it, but seems like when I was a boy I knew someone named that." He shook his head, unable to make the connection. "Tell me what else you learned. Maybe it'll jog my memory."

Rebecca continued to tell Mitch about the episode in Edmund's study and the dream about Sabrina's return to Soquili with Grant. She also related Edmund's confirmation of her dream with the facts about how Soquili had been spared and how Jemima hid the horses inside the house.

"I bet that was a smelly few days!" Mitch chuckled. "Imagine keepin' three o' these fella's inside the house!" Suddenly a memory flashed into Mitch's mind, "You know! I remember distinctly seein' horses inside a house as a child. I mean that's an odd enough thing to witness and I most certainly do remember it. And come to think of it, it was here at Soquili!"

"You do? You were here then?"

"Yeah, my family's house burned to the ground and your Grandma took us in. My parents have always loved her for that."

He paused and she smiled as she thought of her grandmother taking in little Mitch and his family. He continued with the story, "Your Grandma took in a lot of folks – bein' that her house was the only one standin' for miles around. People came and she gave 'em food to eat and a warm place to stay. My parents told me all about it. Those last days o' the war and after it for years people had nothin' – I mean nothin'. Men came home desperate and completely devoid of all hope – nothin' to live for. Their old way of life destroyed, their slaves gone and they had nothin' to rebuild with and had no idea about how to begin again. Your Grandma took folks in and they lived here together, workin' Soquili, livin' through the winter off the oats stored in the barn that would've been fed to the horses that the Union soldiers stole. There were potatoes out in the field too but that was about it."

"Really? How many people lived here?"

"It was about four or five families I think."

"For how long?" Rebecca asked. She couldn't imagine having to share her home with so many people or what it would be like to try to feed them all with oats and potatoes.

"We all stayed through the winter and your Grandma gave a lot of us seed to grow our own gardens on our own property in the spring, but we lived at Soquili. Then folks one-by-one worked together to rebuild their homes. It took a couple years really. People stayed here at Soquili for quite a while until they were able to get on their feet. They worked together and shared what they had. It's the only way families around here survived."

"Amazing!" Rebecca shook her head. "And do you remember this yourself?"

"Well, bits and pieces. I was only about six at the time of the battle and the war was over by April o' the next year. Pa came home then. He was so devastated. Not only had they lost the war, but he'd lost everythin' he'd worked his whole life for – came home to nothin' but desolation. My family stayed here for almost a year before we rebuilt a little cabin to live in. I still 'member workin' here in this very stable to help earn our keep. This wasn't the one that burned. It was a different one that burned and they rebuilt that one a few years later when there were more horses again."

"I had no idea that it was so bad," Rebecca shook her head.

"It was for the grownups, but for me as a kid, it was just fun. I mean, gettin' to live in that big ol' house and be around the horses. Soquili was so much bigger than our place had been that I felt like we were rich gettin' to live here."

"Guess it's all in how you look at it," she smiled.

"Guess so," Mitch looked out the stable door as a loud thunder cracked and a gust of wind blew. The rains descended in a sudden torrential downpour. The horses began to whinny and Mitch ran to close the stable doors, shutting them in and bolting the door securely. He reached over and turned up the light of a lantern that hung from the wall.

"May as well have a seat, Rebecca. I think you're stuck in here for a while." He motioned toward a bail of hay and she sat down on it, rubbing her arms with her hands. "You cold?" he asked.

"Aren't you? You're soaked clean through," she pointed to his damp clothing which clung to his body.

"It is a bit nippy, but I think there's some blankets over here that we use for the horses," he opened a cupboard and pulled out a grey woolen blanket. "Hmmm… just one."

"You take it," she suggested.

"Don't worry. It's clean," he held it open.

"I know, you take it. You've got to be colder than I am. You're soaked to the bone," she observed.

"Nonsense, scoot over," he sat down next to her on the hay and nudged her teasingly. She moved over to give him room and he put the blanket around both of them.

Rebecca's heart pounded as she tried in vain to avoid thinking about how close he sat to her. She felt suddenly tongue-tied, praying in her mind that the storm would cease so she could be free of the unnerving situation. She rubbed both hands nervously on her arms trying to keep moving and avoid the incredible urge she felt to snuggle up next to him under the blanket.

"You still cold?" He put his arm around her and pulled the blanket tighter to keep her warm against his body.

She closed her eyes, unable to believe that her nervous reaction actually encouraged him to take her in his arms. "Have you finished all your work in here?" she blurted out in an effort to get him back up moving around the barn at a safe distance.

"Yep, they've all been brushed, fed and watered. Not much else I can do with all this rain," he mumbled as he glanced over at her. She looked terrified. "You scared o' storms, Becca?" he asked.

"No, why?" she asked, simultaneously wondering why he chose that moment, when they were huddled up next to each other, to shorten her name to something so endearing.

"You look frightened," he smiled, his arm still draped around her shoulder, rubbing her back and arm to keep her warm.

"I'm not frightened. I'm just cold," she forced a smile to avoid further betraying the anxiety raging within her due to being so close to him.

A loud clap of thunder rumbled and lightning struck threateningly close to the stable. Midnight whinnied and reared in his stall, causing Mitch to jump up from the bail of hay to settle him.

"There, there, boy. It's all right," he soothed as he stroked the horse's neck to calm the animal.

Rebecca breathed a sigh of relief and pulled the blanket tightly around her shoulders, leaning over with her face in her hands. *Sparks and magic. What in the world was I thinking?* she thought to herself. If she'd been with Stephen right now, she wouldn't be feeling any of this. The thought of Stephen at that moment caused a fleeting twinge of guilt and at the same time the realization crystallized that she could never marry Stephen when someone else made her feel like this. Why did her father send her home to Soquili? He couldn't have known that...

Rebecca's Reveries

Rebecca opened her eyes to find Mitch's face directly in front of hers as he crouched before her, "You all right, Becca?"

"I'm fine," she felt like she'd melt every time he called her by that name. No one had referred to her as Becca since her father ceased the habit when she turned fourteen. Caroline insisted that a young woman should be called Rebecca. She'd never told her mother that she preferred Becca. Instead she went along with her mother's wishes in an effort to appear grown up and mature. Something about the name Rebecca made her feel prim and proper and required that propriety and decorum be observed, but Becca was a bit mischievous as a youth. She snuck off to ride horses, played out in the fields with her friends when she was supposed to be working and stole prize flowers from her mother's rose garden. She wondered if her mother knew that if Becca became Rebecca she'd settle down and play by the rules.

Mitch brushed a stray lock of her hair into place with his finger and as his hand slid to her cheek a warm thrilling sensation poured over her body replacing the chill that had been there only moments prior. It seemed as if his eyes were bluer than usual as Rebecca gazed into them. She jumped involuntarily as another lightning bolt lit up the sky immediately followed by a loud clap of thunder that seemed to roll on continuously afterward.

He put his arms around her pulling her to him. She rested her head on his shoulder and breathed deeply inhaling the scent of him. "It's all right, Becca. You're safe in here," his voice was low and soothing and he smelled of leather and witch hazel.

"Am I?" she mumbled as she lifted her head and her dark brown eyes met his once more. His gaze descended to her lips. Even if Mitch hadn't taken her face in his strong calloused hand, Rebecca still would have felt no instinctive urge to turn her cheek to him. Instead, her eyes fell to his full bottom lip accented by his thick, yet neatly trimmed mustache which obstructed her view of his upper lip. She remained motionless as he tenderly placed several gentle kisses on her lips. As his attentions to her soft lips deepened, something came over Rebecca that she'd never felt before outside of dreams and she fully engaged herself in his fervent kisses that warmed her from head to toe.

Loud pounding on the stable door startled them and Mitch abruptly broke from her, stood and crossed the stable to unlatch the door, "Mr. Marchant, you're soaked!"

Rebecca rose to her feet, her heart thumping within her chest, with the blanket wrapped securely around her shoulders. "Uncle Edmund" she mumbled as a wave of panic seized her breast and Edmund rushed into the stable. She fully expected him to call her a trollop and send her back to the house.

"What are you doin' out here, child? Your Grandma's been turnin' the house upside down lookin' for ya. She sent me out in this mess to search for ya," Edmund scolded.

"I'm sorry, Uncle Edmund. I didn't mean to frighten anyone or cause trouble," Rebecca apologized.

"She came out to see the horses. And shortly afterward the storm started ragin'. So I closed up the stable to protect us from the elements." Mitch looked over at Rebecca whose face had grown pale. "Your niece is afraid o' storms, I think, Mr. Marchant."

"Well, come along child. It's startin' to subside. Come on in the house before it starts up again. You'll catch your death of cold out here," Edmund motioned for her to join him and she followed without a backward glance at Mitch.

About halfway to the house, Edmund looked back over his shoulder, "You come on inside and dry yourself Mitch. You're soaked to the bone."

Mitch shut the stable doors behind him and jogged toward the house after them.

Chapter 5

"My word, Mitch! You're drenched!" Jemima met them at the door. "Where were you, Rebecca?"

"I was just in the stable. You know me, Grandma, can't stand to be cooped up inside the house for more than a day," Rebecca smiled.

"It started that thunder crackin' downpour so she had to wait in the stable for it to clear," Mitch added.

"Uh huh," Jemima nodded knowingly.

Rebecca's face flushed and she stared at Jemima, her eyes pleading for her grandmother to cease the insinuative remarks while Uncle Edmund was present.

"Well, y'all come on in here and get dried off and eat breakfast," Jemima turned to Mitch, "I believe you've got an extra set of work clothes 'round here someplace don't ya?"

"Yes'm," Mitch walked to the hall closet and retrieved a shirt and a pair of pants that he kept on hand for just such occasions. He carried them into the washroom and shut the door. Rebecca scurried up the stairs to her bedroom to find some dry clothes.

Just as she slipped out of her wet dress and hung it up, she heard a knock at her door. "Yes? Who is it?"

"It's me, dear, Grandma," Jemima answered softly from the other side of the door.

Rebecca crossed to the door and opened it slightly to see what her grandmother wanted, "Yes, Grandma?"

Jemima entered the room carrying two fresh towels and Rebecca, who wore only her corset and petticoats, quickly shut the door. "Here, I thought you could use some fresh linen." Jemima plopped down on Rebecca's bed.

"Thank you," Rebecca placed one towel on her dresser while she opened the other and patted her arms, neck and hair dry. Jemima just sat there smiling. "Can I help you with somethin', Grandma?" Rebecca asked quizzically.

"Yeah, you can tell me what really happened in the stable this mornin'," Jemima winked.

"What?" Rebecca's face flushed crimson.

"Never mind," Jemima rose and crossed to the door, "you just answered my question." She put her hand on the doorknob and then turned her head back toward Rebecca as the smile faded from her lips and her expression became serious, "Be careful darlin'. It's fire you're playin' with."

"What?" Rebecca shook her head, "Really, Grandma, I don't know what you're talkin' about."

"I think you do, Rebecca. Come on down for breakfast when you're dressed."

Rebecca stood staring at the door, and then her mouth dropped open astonished by what her grandmother insinuated. She was so perturbed that her grandmother would think her capable of such a thing that she huffed, thrust her hands to her hips and stared at her wet hair in the mirror.

"Good grief!" she muttered to herself. Grabbing a fresh dress, she slipped into it. Standing before the mirror, she fidgeted with her long wet hair trying to decide how to arrange it when she began to feel light headed. At first she thought another vision was stirring, but as the dizziness faded, she found herself still standing before the mirror arranging her hair in a fashion she'd never tried before. Normally Rebecca wore her hair down or in braids or a ponytail. But as another wave of dizziness hit her she found herself standing before her bedroom mirror with her hair parted on the side, elegantly swept up and arranged neatly on the top of her head so that it accentuated her long slender neck. Rebecca stared at herself, mystified as to how she had managed to arrange her hair so beautifully.

By the time Rebecca made it downstairs to the dining room, everyone sat around the table and Hilda carried plates of food setting them before each person. Just as Rebecca gracefully entered the room with her hair swept up in a stunning fashion, Hilda carried Mitch's plate from the kitchen. The second Hilda saw her, she dropped the plate and it shattered on the hardwood floor – fried eggs, bacon and broken china mingled at her feet. Hilda just stood there with her mouth hanging open in Rebecca's direction with the whites of her eyes as big as saucers.

Edmund, Jemima and Mitch turned in unison toward the shattered plate, up toward Hilda and then their heads followed her gaze straight to Rebecca. Edmund's and Jemima's mouths dropped open and Mitch's eyebrows rose at her breath-taking beauty, but he had no idea why everyone else glared at her with their mouths dropped open. He

instantly rose from his seat and looked back and forth
between Rebecca and Hilda who had now stooped down to
clean up the mess. He finally decided on pulling out the chair
next to himself for Rebecca to be seated, but instead of sitting
Rebecca went to Hilda and assisted her with the mess. Mitch
stooped beside her helping Hilda with the bits of shattered
china.

"You two youngins sit down, I'll get this. I'm gettin'
clumsy in my old age," Hilda rose and nodded toward
Jemima and Edmund, "I'm sorry. I'll get this cleaned right
up." The shaken woman scurried into the kitchen and
shortly returned with a broom, dustpan and wash cloth.

Mitch and Rebecca carried the pieces of glass they held
in their hands to the kitchen to discard them while Hilda
cleaned up the mess in the dining room.

"What in the world was that about?" Rebecca whispered
once the kitchen door swung shut.

"I think it was you," his eyes studied her new hair style.

"Me?"

"Yes, you look … well you look gorgeous… but you look
even more familiar to me now," he put his hand to his chin
and stared at her pensively.

"Stop starin' at me like that," she whispered and her eyes
darted to the door where Hilda entered carrying a dustpan
full of china and food. Rebecca quickly turned to wash her
hands in a pan of sudsy water on the counter.

"She is breath-takin' with her hair like that, don't you
think, Miss Hilda?" Mitch suddenly addressed the servant
who nervously discarded the contents of the dustpan.

"Huh?" Hilda looked up at Mitch.

"That's why you dropped the plate isn't it? She just takes your breath away with her hair arranged like that," he pointed toward Rebecca and her face turned crimson.

"Oh, yes, she is very lovely with her hair like that, but I – I'm just clumsy's all." Hilda left the kitchen to finish her cleaning.

"Why did you say that?" Rebecca asked him in irritation.

"I felt sorry for the old woman and well, it's true," he shrugged his shoulders as his eyes followed the contours of her bare neck which had before remained hidden behind her long flowing hair.

Rebecca sighed with disbelief and rolled her eyes as she quickly exited the kitchen and Mitch followed her back to the table, pulling her chair out for her. Rebecca glanced toward her grandmother and uncle who appeared to have collected themselves, but still studied her oddly.

"Why is everyone lookin' at me that way?" Rebecca finally burst out as her eyes moved from person to person.

"She looks familiar somehow. Don't you think Mr. and Mrs. Marchant?" Mitch prodded as he leaned his elbow on the table and stared at her resting his head on his fist. His constant reference to her appearance in front of her relatives completely rattled her.

"No," Edmund shook his head, his full bottom lip protruding as if he had no idea to what Mitch referred.

Jemima shook her head negatively and shrugged her shoulders, "No, but you do look lovely dear. I don't believe I've ever seen you wear your hair like that."

"I haven't. I – uh – I just felt like wearing it differently today, but if it's going to make people drop plates and gawk, I'll go back to my braids or loose locks."

"Oh no, I like it this way," Mitch smiled.

"Yes, I bet you do," Edmund mumbled sarcastically under his breath as an expression of irritation furrowed his brow.

"Well, Hilda, let's get Mitch another plate, shall we please?," Jemima called exuberantly in an effort to change the subject.

Hilda scurried from the kitchen carrying two more plates and set them before Mitch and Rebecca, "I'm sorry for the mess, Ma'am. I'll be more careful in the future."

"Yes, please do that," Edmund muttered.

"It's all right, Hilda, accidents happen, dear," Jemima smiled kindly at the servant and shot Edmund an irritated glare as Hilda left the room.

The tension was as thick as buttermilk throughout the remainder of the meal and Rebecca just wanted to escape. Edmund took his last bite and stood, flinging his napkin into his seat behind him, "I'll be in my study if anyone needs me." He started for the door and then turned back abruptly, "Oh and Mitch, stop by and see me before you leave today. We have some business to review."

"Yes, Sir," Mitch nodded and Edmund left the room.

Jemima yawned, putting her hand over her mouth, "I'm sorry, dears. I'm still not feelin' too well. I think I better go lie down." She rose from her seat and Mitch stood.

Rebecca stood as Jemima left the table, "Can I get anything for you, Grandma?"

117

"No thank you dear, I'm fine. I just need to lie down and rest," she called over her shoulder as she left the room.

Rebecca reached over and began stacking the plates to clear the table and Mitch assisted her. As he entered the kitchen Mitch suggested, "Miss Hilda, why don't you go take a rest yourself. Miss Marchant and I can take care of the dishes."

"Are you sure?" Hilda hesitated.

"Certainly, go lie down. You don't look like you feel well," Rebecca agreed.

"Yes, you look as if you've seen a ghost or somethin'" Mitch added.

"Well, I think I may go lie down just a little while. Thank you for helpin'," Hilda left them to attend to the dishes.

After a few moments, Rebecca went to the door and peered out making sure that Hilda was gone, then suddenly turned toward Mitch, "What in the world were you tryin' to do?"

"What do you mean?" Mitch shrugged his shoulders innocently.

"Oh, come on! What was all that 'she's so breath-taking' and 'she looks so familiar' nonsense. You were up to somethin' with all that, weren't you?"

A broad mischievous grin spread across his handsome face, "It's obvious you triggered somethin' with your entrance. You saw their expressions didn't you? I was just tryin' to get someone to fess up to whatever's goin' on 'round here."

"You think somethin's goin' on?"

"It's obvious ain't it? You turn up with all these memories of people and places you've never known and your entire family denies it, yet they act like they've seen a ghost when you enter the room. Somethin's up, Becca. They're tryin' to keep somethin' from you. That's as plain as the nose on your pretty little face."

Her gaze dropped nervously to her feet. His going on about her beauty made her intensely uncomfortable. Mitch stepped closer toward her and put his hand on her chin, lifting her eyes to look into his and his hand slipped cradling the softness of her long neck. "And you are breath-takin' Becca. That's just the simple truth."

She stepped nervously back away from him, all but fleeing into the dining room to gather silverware and glasses.

Chuckling, he took some dishes from the counter and plunged them into the dishwater. She carried the dishes back into the kitchen and set them on the counter next to him.

"I didn't mean to scare ya, Becca," he apologized.

"You didn't scare me, for heaven's sake," she muttered.

"I didn't –eh? Then why did ya bolt like a scared rabbit?" he chuckled.

"My mother taught me that too much flattery is a sign that someone's up to no good," she answered resolutely.

"Oh, so you're sayin' I'm up to no good, am I?" he teased, drying his hand on a towel. "If I'm no good, then you can just finish these dishes yourself!" he winked and left the kitchen.

"Great! Volunteer us for the job and then leave me to finish it!" she huffed and plunged a dish into the soapy water. As she washed dishes, Rebecca pondered on the fuss everyone had made and wondered why her hair style had triggered such a reaction. They did act as if they'd seen a ghost. Maybe she did look like someone they all knew, but who? Just as she dried the last dish and placed it in the cupboard, Mitch abruptly entered the kitchen.

"Why *did* you decide to fix your hair that way?" he blurted out.

"Huh?" she turned around to look at him.

"Why did you fix your hair that way?" His expression was so serious that he caught her off guard.

"Uh, I don't know. Why?" He didn't reply so she continued, "Why are you suddenly comin' in here asking me about this? What's goin' on?"

"Because I think I know why everyone's mouths flew open and Hilda dropped the plate when you entered the room. But I want you to tell me why you fixed your hair that way first," he answered.

"I really don't know, Mitch. I thought you said everyone acted that way because I'm so *breath-taking*," she quipped sarcastically.

"You are!" he grinned and then the seriousness in his expression returned. "But there's more to it than that. Surely you know what motivated you to fix your hair like that," he insisted as his eyes roamed over her hair, face and neck.

"I was upstairs tryin' to decide whether to put it in a ponytail or braids when I felt dizzy like another vision was comin' on, but it didn't and I just began arranging my hair like this. I've never even thought to style it this way before and I don't know why I did today."

"So you really don't know why you did it?" he prodded.

"No," she sighed. "I really don't. What is it? Just tell me!"

"It's – It's," he stammered. "It's Sabrina, Rebecca," he whispered excitedly. "You look *exactly* like her with your hair arranged like that. You look *exactly* like her, Becca! Sabrina always fixed her hair like that. That's why you looked so familiar to me."

"So you're sayin' you remember her now?" Mitch nodded affirmatively. "Then who is she? Tell me, Mitch! Who is she?"

"She's a young woman I knew as a child when our family lived here at the end of the war and just afterward. I remember her playin' hide and seek with us and keepin' us entertained. She was so beautiful and had such a happy way about her," Mitch paused, remembering fond memories from his childhood.

"Where is she now?" Rebecca asked.

"She – I don't know. One day she was just gone. I remember lookin' all over for her in the house, the stables and around the farm and she was nowhere. I asked my mother about her and even your grandmother and they just said that she had to leave. I remember being so hurt that she didn't even tell me goodbye."

"And no one told you where she went?" Rebecca asked.

"No, they wouldn't tell me, just that she wouldn't be comin' back any time soon. I never saw her again. That seems like a lifetime ago. I'd forgotten all about her until this afternoon."

"So who was she? Was she a servant?"

"No, she wasn't a servant. I think …" he paused. "I think she was your Grandma's daughter!" his eyes widened in recollection. "Yes! She's your aunt, Becca! She's Edmund's sister!"

"Really?"

"Why of course! It makes total sense. You look just like her and both of you look like Mrs. Marchant. Plus, think of Edmund's reaction in the stable to finding her with Grant. Think of her discussing Grant's reasons for joining the Union. And the way Jemima treated her when I was young. Yes, I'm positive she's your aunt!"

"I wonder what happened to her. And why is everyone so secretive about her?"

"I don't know," Mitch shook his head.

Rebecca's eyes widened as she looked up at him. "Maybe she died and they didn't have the heart to tell you since you were such a small child."

"Maybe... very well could be..."

Rebecca opened the kitchen door and walked out. Mitch followed her through the dining room, into the living room and just as she was about to go through the double doors into the foyer, Mitch whispered, "Where're you goin'?" She motioned for him to follow her as she went out the front door onto the porch.

"Let's sit out here for a spell and figure this out. No one should be able to hear us out here," she suggested.

They rocked in silence, watching the drizzling rain descend. "So what now?" she finally spoke.

"I have an idea," Mitch rubbed his chin. "And I think it just might work." A mischievous grin spread across his face.

"What is it?"

"What if I confront your uncle Edmund about it?" he suggested.

"What? What would you say?"

"Well, think about it. It's obvious they all made a fuss over your appearance. They can't deny that they did. And I even said you looked familiar at breakfast. The memories did come back to me quite naturally because of the situation. So if I mention the similarities between you two, it'll be quite natural. But if you say somethin', they won't know how you connected the dots."

"I guess... but they could think you told me after you realized."

"I have a feelin' that might make them mad. I mean if they don't want you to know and they find out I told you... You see what I mean?"

"So this way, they'll think I'm still in the dark about it all and we won't be divulging everything I know."

"Exactly. You'll still be free to snoop around and solve the mystery. But if we're lucky, Edmund might reveal somethin' to me that he wouldn't reveal to you."

"I'd imagine he'll swear you to secrecy on the matter. Then what?"

"We'll just continue to pretend that you don't know."

Rebecca sighed, "This is getting complicated."

"But I think it's worth the risk, don't you?"

"I don't know, Mitch. Edmund has quite a temper," Rebecca shook her head.

"Oh, he's as passive as a lamb. I've never once seen him riled."

"I have!" Rebecca rolled her eyes.

"You have? Really? I can't imagin' him gettin' riled," Mitch looked astonished.

"Well, it was in the past... in my reveries," Rebecca answered.

"I think he's changed since then. He doesn't seem anything like the man he was."

"But he's capable... Mitch... you better watch your step," she warned.

"Yeah, he might get mad and swat a fly in front of me," Mitch chuckled and leaned back in his rocker, closing his eyes. "Don't you just love the sound o' the rain? Makes me feel like takin' a nap," he rocked with his eyes closed and his head leaned back.

"Yes, it is relaxing. But right now I've got too many questions runnin' through my mind to relax."

"We'll figure it all out soon enough," he calmly assured, "Just be patient."

"Patience never has been one of my virtues," she mumbled. She closed her eyes and replayed in her mind everything she knew about Sabrina searching for clues as to what happened to her, but thought of nothing new. When she opened her eyes again, Mitch had gone to sleep in the rocker. The situation gave her an opportunity to examine him closely.

He was unbelievably handsome. Whereas most men of the day wore beards, Mitch kept his face clean shaven except for a neatly trimmed blonde mustache which was slightly darker than his short sun-streaked blonde hair that parted on the side. His side burns extended accentuating his defined cheekbones, masculine square jaw and full lips. She thought

124

back to earlier that morning and what it had felt like to be kissed by those warm soft lips, his mustache tickling the corners of her mouth. *Does he really think I'm beautiful?* The question popped into her mind. She had been furious with him when he'd said it before because she thought he was just teasing her or egging on her relatives to pry information from them. But just inside hadn't he said that Sabrina was beautiful and that Rebecca looked just like her. But he'd also said Sabrina had a happy way about her. Maybe it was her way that made her beautiful.

Mitch stirred and his head turned toward her, his long eyelashes moved and the corner of his mouth twitched. Thinking he'd awaken and find her staring at him she quickly directed her gaze out toward the yard were the rain had ceased and the sun started to peek through the clouds.

Mitch yawned, stretching his long arms high above his head and then slapped his calloused hands to his thighs, "Well, it looks like it's lettin' up."

"I hope so," Rebecca leaned forward to better inspect the sky.

"I better go see what your Uncle Edmund wanted and head home before it starts up again," he rose to his feet and adjusted his suspenders on his broad shoulders and rolled up his white shirtsleeves exposing his golden brown muscular forearms.

"You'll tell me what he says before you leave?" she looked up at him anxiously.

"Oh, sure. If it feels like the right time, I'll ask him and let you know what I learn," he winked at her.

"Good luck," she told him as he put his hand on the doorknob.

"Thanks," he smiled and disappeared within the house. Rebecca decided to wait outside on the porch for him.

Mitch tapped lightly on Edmund's study door, "Sir, may I come in?"

"Oh, yes, come in, Mitch," Edmund replied.

A wave of cigar smoke hit Mitch's nostrils as he entered the smoky study to find Edmund sitting at his desk reviewing paperwork.

"You said you wanted to speak with me about business?" Mitch stood in front of Edmund's desk.

"Yes, have a seat," Edmund pointed to a chair in front of the desk.

Mitch sat down and crossed his leg, propping his right ankle on his left knee. He watched Edmund as he continued to read over a sheet of paper and mark several spots with ink. After a few minutes had passed in silence, Edmund looked up to Mitch.

"Mr. Ingles of Athens has purchased the four horses that he looked at last week. Jefferson and I will deliver them to him in the morning. So I'll need you to prepare them to go.

"Yes, Sir," Mitch nodded.

"Also, Mrs. Phelps wants her daughter to take riding lessons. It looks like your schedule is free on Thursdays at three, am I right?"

"Yes, Sir, that'll be fine."

"How's the Appaloosa comin' along?"

"She's progressing nicely, should give birth within the week, I'd say," Mitch answered.

"Good, good, I've already got a buyer for the foal when it's ready," Edmund seemed pleased and then went back to his stack of papers.

After several moments of silence, Mitch asked, "Was there anything else you needed from me, Sir?"

"Yes," Edmund held up his index finger while he continued to read the paper, "One more thing." He finished perusing the paper and then folded his arms across the desk in front of him. "I have a favor to ask."

"Yes, Sir, anything." Mitch nodded.

"I'd like for you to reduce the time you spend with my niece," his voice and face showed no emotion and Mitch wasn't sure how to take the request.

"What exactly do you mean, Sir?" Mitch's eyebrows puckered.

"To put it plainly, I don't want you two getting romantically involved," he stated flatly.

Mitch shook his head and shrugged his shoulders, "What makes you think that we're getting romantically involved?"

"I have eyes, Mr. Garrison. I don't want her getting hurt," he still showed not a shred of emotion.

"I have no intention of hurting your niece, Sir," Mitch assured.

"While she's in my care, I must insist that you keep your distance from her," Edmund looked back down at his papers as if the discussion had concluded.

"This wouldn't have to do with Sabrina would it?" Mitch decided that now was the time to confront Edmund. "She looks just like her don't you think?"

Edmund's head popped up and something akin to fear clouded his eyes for a split second before the bland haze rolled back over them. He leaned back in his chair. "What are you drivin' at, Mitch?"

"I just mean, I know the story about Sabrina and Grant and with how much Rebecca looks like her, are you worried something similar will happen here between Rebecca and myself? Because, I assure you, Sir, I am an honorable man and I would never take advantage of your niece."

Edmund rose from his seat, "I'd prefer that you kept your knowledge of Sabrina and Grant to yourself. Rebecca's parents didn't want her to be aware of the whole sordid situation. They went to great lengths to keep Rebecca shielded from the world and I won't have her contaminated on my watch."

Mitch stood, "I assure you, Sir, I have no intention of contaminating your niece."

Edmund's voice lowered, "I'm sorry, Mitch. I didn't mean to insinuate that you would. I'd hoped she'd tell you this herself, but Rebecca's engaged to be married to a young man in Kentucky. His family is well-respected in the horse-breeding business and her Aunt Miriam assures me that he is a fine young man who will make a good husband for Rebecca. It's my intention to see that she returns to this young man as innocent as the way she came here. Do I make myself clear?"

Mitch felt like someone hit him in the stomach, "Yes, Sir. You make yourself abundantly clear. Thank you for apprising me of the situation. May I go now, Sir?"

"Yes, you may go," Edmund nodded and sat back down to his papers.

Mitch started for the front door and then realizing that Rebecca still sat out on the porch waiting for him, he turned and stomped through the house, out the back door, mounted his horse and rode home the back way so that she never saw him leave.

Rebecca waited for nearly an hour on the front porch and when Mitch never came out, she decided to see if he was still inside. Finding him nowhere, she went out to the stables and discovered that his horse was gone. A sick feeling spread over her for fear that her uncle had fired him when he confronted him about Sabrina. But then she remembered that he said he'd discuss it if it felt like the right time. Maybe he didn't get a chance to confront Edmund and decided to go home while the rain had still stopped. As she walked back to the house, it began to sprinkle again and she picked up the pace, quickly entering the back door.

For the rest of the afternoon and evening, Rebecca vacillated between worrying about Mitch and assuring herself that he had just gone home before the rains returned. At dinner with the family, no one said another word about her hair or anything about Mitch's abrupt departure. Rebecca retired to her bedroom early, putting another log on the fire, creating a cozy, warm glow. Deep in thought about her aunt Sabrina and her encounter with Mitch that morning, she settled into a rocker in front of the fire, staring at the orange and yellow flame and enjoying the warmth from it. She soon drifted into one of her reveries of the past.

Sabrina flung her arms around him and his full beard tickled her neck as he leaned over embracing her. "However did you manage to slip away?" she asked as she tugged both of his hands, leading him into the stable and shutting the door behind them.

"We're trying to take Chattanooga. With the railroad runnin' through here, it's a strategic point. We need to block off supplies to the South. They sent me to carry a message to Rosecrans here at Chickamauga. I delivered my message and thought they'd never know if I stopped off here and spent a little time with my favorite girl," he winked.

"Oh Grant! I've missed you so much!" she hugged him, kissing his cheeks.

"You have no idea how much I've wanted to see you again. The vision of your beautiful face is all that has helped me survive this wretched war." He caressed her cheek with his rough hand and kissed her lips.

He began rummaging through his vest pocket. "I – uh, I have somethin' for you."

He dropped to one knee in front of her and held out a small gold ring with two interlocking hearts, "You are the love of my life, Sabrina. You're all I live for. Will you marry me, my love? When this war is over, will you be my bride?"

She fell to her knees in front of him and embraced his neck, "Oh Grant! Yes, I'll marry you!" He took her left hand in his, and she watched him slip the ring on her finger.

Rebecca looked down at her hands. Sabrina's heart ring encircled the ring finger of her right hand. Her parents had given it to her on her sixteenth birthday. Something must have happened to Sabrina. If she were alive, wouldn't she still be wearing her ring? Why would she allow it to be given to a niece she'd never seen. With the realization that Sabrina must indeed be dead, tears welled in Rebecca's eyes. She had come to love the young woman she had only met in her dreams. She'd felt so much of what Sabrina felt and experienced so many pivotal moments in her life that she mourned the loss of her dear young aunt whom she would never have the opportunity to meet.

Rebecca rose from the rocker, dabbing the tears from her eyes with her handkerchief. She stood in front of the mirror, staring at her reflection – Sabrina's reflection. She reached up and let down hair, letting it flow around her shoulders. She may look like Sabrina, but she wasn't Sabrina inside. She'd had a glimpse of Sabrina's heart and the young girl who felt so deeply, loved so much and suffered so greatly was dead and Rebecca determined never again to cause her family pain by wearing her hair like Sabrina. She changed into her nightgown and climbed into bed.

The next morning dawned bright and clear and having experienced a restful slumber void of disturbing dreams, Rebecca awoke rejuvenated. She rushed to the window to look out. A relieved smile spread across her face as she saw Mitch entering the stable, mud clinging to the bottom of his boots from the saturating rains. Quickly, she dressed and descended the stairs. Determining that she still had some time before breakfast, she slipped out the back door and made her way to the stable, the wet grass clinging to her shoes. She breathed deeply of the aroma of wet hay and fresh clean air.

Mitch seemed entrenched in thought as he stooped over, repairing a brown mare's shoe. So engrossed in his task was he, that he didn't notice Rebecca's approach. She leaned her elbows against the stall and watched him work, his strong arms flexing as he held the horse's hoof in one hand and hammered the shoe in place with the other. He didn't notice her for several minutes and without thinking she found herself mesmerized by his muscular arms and his clenched jaw as he concentrated on his task. Suddenly he looked up, "Oh," he jumped a little, "Didn't your parents ever teach you that it's impolite to sneak up on somebody?" he snapped in irritation, his brow wrinkling with disturbance.

"I – I'm sorry," she began to back away. "I didn't mean to disturb you," she apologized, thoroughly embarrassed and turning to leave.

He quickly slipped out of the stall and caught her by the arm, "Wait."

With the warmth of his strong hand firmly encircling her arm, Rebecca's heart raced with exhilaration akin to what Sabrina experienced in Grant's arms that fateful morning in the stable, and it frightened her. Quickly she pulled her arm from his hand.

"And your parents should've taught you that it's rude to grab a woman in such a rough manner!" she retorted as she walked briskly back toward the house.

Mitch stood there hesitating, watching her go until suddenly determination registered in his jaw and he jogged after her, grabbed both of her shoulders from behind and turned her around to face him.

"I'm sorry, I didn't mean to snap at you. You just startled me's all."

"Well, I'm sorry. It won't happen again," she spat. There was that adrenaline rush again and all Rebecca wanted to do was run – to be free of his intoxicating presence. She wiggled, trying to free herself from his grasp, but he still held her securely by her shoulders. "Let me go, Mitch," she pleaded.

"What's goin' on? Why are you actin' like this?" he searched her eyes with his. She looked like a scared deer ready to bolt.

"Me? You're the one who got all bent out of shape just 'cause I didn't announce myself the minute I entered the stable – just because I didn't want to disturb your work!"

His voice softened and his chiseled features began to relax, "I'm sorry, Miss Marchant. I shouldn't have snapped at you. I didn't mean to frighten you."

"You didn't *frighten* me, *Mr. Garrison*," the defensiveness began to rise again in her eyes. "I simply am not accustomed to men snapping at me or handling me so roughly." She looked to her shoulders which were still covered by his calloused bronze hands.

Before she could lift her gaze from her shoulders, his right hand held her chin securely directing her gaze upward into his eyes, she could feel his warm breath on her lips and her knees began to buckle. Expecting that his lips would meet hers at any instant, so close were they that she could feel the warmth emanating from them, she closed her eyes.

"Maybe you're not frightened of me, Rebecca. Maybe you're frightened of yourself when you're with me." Suddenly he released his grip on her chin and shoulder, turned and stomped back to the stable. "When you're ready to be honest with me, you know where to find me," he called back over his shoulder and disappeared into the stable.

Rebecca clenched her fists in irritation and groaned, "The gall!" She spun around and stomped into the house.

Chapter 6

Rebecca and Mitch kept their distance from one another for a week — Mitch, following Uncle Edmund's orders, and Rebecca too stubborn to admit her attraction for him. Finally, one October evening, the family had eaten dinner and the sun set in the western sky in a blaze of pinks, purples and light blue blasts. Rebecca stood at her bedroom window and noticed Mitch milling around by the stable.

"Be honest with him? Be honest about what?" she muttered to herself. "What does he expect me to say? You make my knees weak? You make me forget that I have a rich man and a diamond ring waiting for me back home? Or perhaps 'Oh Mitch you're so handsome and strong take me away to be your bride!' she rolled her eyes sarcastically. Afraid of myself when I'm with him! The nerve! I have a good mind to go buy my ticket home tomorrow!"

She turned abruptly and stomped out of her room and down the corridor to Jemima's bedroom, knocking soundly on the door. Jemima answered, "Yes, who is it?"

"It's me, Grandma, may I come in?" Rebecca called.

"Certainly, dear."

Rebecca entered the room and stood in front of her grandmother who sat in her rocker sewing. "Grandma, I think it's time for me to go back to Kentucky."

"What? So soon? You've barely even been here two weeks!" Jemima dropped her sewing to her lap.

"Well, I don't mean this minute, but I was thinking of purchasing my ticket for next week," Rebecca answered.

"Oh, stay a little longer. I get to see you so rarely and we've only just started to get to know each other again!" Jemima pleaded.

"Grandma, I have no idea why Papa told me to come back here or what he expected me to learn or discover, but it's been the most confusing trip of my life," she flung her arms in the air in frustration.

"What are you talkin' about, dear? What do you mean your father wanted you to come back here? And why is it confusin'?"

"Papa's dying words to me were that I should come back here before I made my decision about Stephen Phillips' marriage proposal. He made it sound like there was somethin' he should've said or done and that by comin' back here I'd be able to figure it out. But the only thing I've figured out is that people can make some really big mistakes when they let emotions rule their will and that it hurts abominably when you lose someone you love."

Rebecca knew what it was like to lose a parent, but she hadn't fully comprehended what it would be like to lose a man she loved like Sabrina loved Grant.

"Those sound like some valuable lessons, but how, pray tell, did you learn them in your short stay here?"

"It's a long story," Rebecca sighed.

"Well, you're not leavin' for another week, surely we have enough time for you to tell me," Jemima smiled encouragingly.

"I don't know, Grandma. You'll think I'm crazy," Rebecca shook her head in frustration.

"No I won't, dear. Would this have to do with Mitch or the way you two've been avoidin' one another for the last week?"

"What makes you think we're avoiding one another?" Rebecca plopped down on her grandmother's bed.

"You two were nearly inseparable the first few days you were here and now you mope around the house and he mopes around the stable. He's been a horrible grump. Jefferson said he saw him slammin' things around in the stable muttering to himself about dishonest women."

"*Dishonest women!* He has a lot of nerve!" Rebecca clenched her fists and jaw.

"What's this all about, Rebecca? What's goin' on between you and Mitch? You can tell me," Jemima's eyes pleaded with Rebecca to confide in her.

Rebecca sighed, "We had an argument and for some reason he's accusin' me of being dishonest with him. But I have no idea why." She flopped back on the bed, lying with her hair flowing about her, her legs dangling off the bed.

"Are you in love with Mitch, and you're thinking you've lost him? Is that what you meant about it hurtin' abominably when you lose someone ya love?"

Rebecca chuckled nervously and sat up leaning on her elbows, "Me? In love with Mitch? To hear him tell it I'm so

137

enamored with him that I don't trust myself in his presence! But no, trust me, that's *not* where I learned that lesson."

"Then I'm confused, child."

"Grandma, I know all about Sabrina and Grant and I suppose y'all wanted to keep it from me because it was tragic and they did things they shouldn't have done, but really I'm old enough to get married myself now and I don't see why everyone has to lie and make it so clandestine," she rolled her eyes in agitation.

"What?" Jemima sat on the edge of her seat. "How do you know about Sabrina and Grant? What do you know and who told you?"

"Nobody had to tell me, Grandma. I've lived Sabrina's life for the last two weeks."

Jemima just stared at her in confusion.

"The first four or five days after I arrived I had continual visions and dreams about Sabrina's life. I've vicariously lived her life, experienced her feelings, her pains and passions. I've had waking visions and sleeping dreams where I'm Sabrina and live moments from her life. Grant proposed to *me*. *I* was with him in the stable. *I* felt her horrid guilt and anguish. It was *me* that Edmund yelled at and called a trollop and sent off to the house, demanding that Grant should do the right thing. *I* found Grant at Snodgrass Hill. *I* carried him back on horseback to this boarded up house. You pulled off the boards to let me in. We hid the horses in the house, the stable was smolderin' and the Union soldiers stole all the horses but Midnight and a couple mares."

"What do you mean *you* did all those things?" Jemima stared at her with a shocked expression on her face.

"Grandma, I've had dreams and visions about Sabrina's life, but in these visions and dreams, I'm her. I feel what she felt, I did what she did and I know first hand what it feels like to succumb to temptation, to love somebody so much that your heart shatters in a million pieces when he's ripped from your life. I know what it feels like to watch your world cave in around you as life as you know it turns into a nightmare." Tears rolled down Rebecca's cheeks. "I know now, Grandma, how wrong I've been to judge people so harshly. If I'd known Sabrina in person, I would've looked down on her as so much dust under my feet. I've always felt that girls like her were the lowest form of life, but I know now that Sabrina was a kind hearted, loving young woman who in a weak moment let her emotions rule her will. She made a mistake which I'm sure she regretted all her life." Rebecca pulled her handkerchief from her pocket and dabbed at the tears.

Jemima rose from her seat and crossed to the window, staring in silence for several minutes, then finally spoke, "Well, I don't regret it."

"What? You *wanted* Sabrina to … to succumb to temptation?" Rebecca asked incredulously.

"No, I didn't wish it upon her, but it always surprises me how God can make a miracle out of our mistakes."

"A miracle out of our mistakes?" Rebecca's eyes grew puzzled.

"You evidently haven't experienced *all* of Sabrina's memories yet, have you, dear?"

"No, I'm sure I haven't, but what do you mean?"

"Perhaps I shouldn't tell you. Perhaps I should let God show you himself through your visions and dreams. Maybe it's somethin' you need to experience to understand," Jemima looked sympathetically at her granddaughter.

"But I haven't had any dreams or visions since… well since the day I wore my hair like Sabrina and everyone acted so shocked. Maybe they've stopped." Rebecca explained.

"God doesn't speak to us when there's malice in our hearts, Rebecca," Jemima sat back down in her rocker and resumed her sewing.

Flopping her head back on the bed, Rebecca thought for a moment and muttered, "You're sayin' I have to make my peace with Mitch?"

"Swallow your pride, Rebecca." Jemima advised.

"Why can't you just tell me the missin' piece?"

"If the visions and dreams don't resume within a few days of your resolving things with Mitch, then I'll tell you," Jemima answered.

"I think you're just tryin' to play matchmaker or somethin'," Rebecca sat up and smiled at Jemima who returned a sly grin. "Maybe I am, but I think Someone higher than myself is doin' a better job of it."

Rebecca rose and crossed to her grandmother's side, "Thank you, Grandma, for not thinking I'm crazy."

"You should've known I'd believe you, dear. You're talkin' to a Cherokee, ya know. If anyone knows the value of walkin' a mile in another girl's moccasins, we do!"

"Oh, I hadn't thought of that," she leaned over and kissed Jemima's cheek. "I love you, Grandma."

"Love you too, dear. Now run along. Sweep your heart clean and make room for more lessons."

Rebecca walked slowly to the door and down the stairs wondering as she went what she could say to Mitch to repair the situation. What did he want from her? Did she have to admit her feelings for him? She wasn't even sure what those feelings were.

When she finally reached the stable, Mitch leaned over the Appaloosa, feeling the horse's stomach as it released a painful whinny.

"Is the foal comin'?" she asked as she knelt next to the horse.

"It's soon. Her water just broke," he rolled up his sleeves.

"Mitch, I came to apologize about the other day."

"Oh?" it wasn't what he expected to hear. "Well, I'm sorry about that too."

"What did you mean about my not bein' honest with you?" she studied him intently.

He worked silently, not sure how to respond then finally spoke, "Why didn't you tell me that you're to be married?"

"What?" her shocked voice rose higher than normal. "Whatever gave you the idea that I'm gettin' married?"

Mitch stood and retrieved a bottle of iodine and bandages. "Don't play dumb with me, Miss Marchant. Your uncle told me all about the rich horse breeder that you're goin' back to Kentucky to marry."

"I didn't know Uncle Edmund even knew about that," she muttered more to herself than to Mitch.

"Well, he did know about it. And it's a good thing he told me, cause you sure didn't!" he lowered his irritated voice to a whisper in an effort not to startle the mare.

"It was simply a proposal which I never accepted. I'm not engaged, Mitch. I promise you that. He asked and I said I'd think about it, but I never said yes."

He looked at her as if she were lying and then began tying back the horse's tail to keep it from interfering with the birthing process.

"Honest, Mitch. I never accepted the proposal. I came here to Soquili because my father told me to come here before I made my decision on the proposal. I even gave back the ring."

"But evidently you planned to. You wouldn't even be here if your father hadn't told you to come here first."

"If I'd stayed in Kentucky, I don't know what I would have decided." she admitted. "But now that I'm here..." she stopped herself.

"Go on... now that you're here..." he crouched between Rebecca and the horse, staring at Rebecca intently.

"I've decided to reject the proposal," she answered.

"Why?" he moved a little closer to her.

Her heart began to beat faster and her palms to sweat. Should she tell him the whole truth or only part of it? Should she admit that she never felt for Stephen what she felt for him? Should she tell him that she couldn't in all honesty agree to marry Stephen when another man made her knees weak, her heart flutter and her mouth water for his kisses? Before she could answer, the horse stirred and whinnied in obvious pain. Mitch turned toward the mare and Rebecca instinctively moved to pat the horses' neck soothingly.

"Looks like there's a hoof comin' through," Mitch moved to the horse's hind quarters.

"Do you see the other one?" Rebecca asked.

"No," he rolled up his sleeve and reached in to gently pull the foal's other hoof through. "I've got it," he said as the second hoof became visible. Within a few minutes, the foal's head began to emerge and the mare groaned as the shoulders followed.

"You're doin' great, girl," Rebecca gently rubbed the mare's neck. Within a few more minutes, the foal had completely emerged. Rebecca handed Mitch a towel to clean the foal.

"Can you please hand me that twine over there so I can tie up the cord," Mitch pointed in the direction of the twine.

"Here," she handed it to him. When he'd finished tying the umbilical cord he sat back and waited for the mare to pass the placenta.

"They're so cute when they're first born, don't you think?" she observed as the foal nursed at its mother's side.

"Uh huh," he nodded as he dried his hands on a clean towel and then rested his forearms over his knees.

"So you never answered my question," he cocked his head and studied her quizzically.

"What question is that?"

"Why have you decided to turn down the rich horseman's proposal?"

She hesitated for a moment, "Oh, look, here comes the rest." Relieved, she pointed toward the horse. Mitch moved closer to the mare.

"Make sure it's all there. You don't want her settin' up infection," she advised.

"I know, I know…" he muttered.

143

Rebecca was grateful for the diversion so that she had time to search for an answer to his question that wouldn't reveal too much of what she'd been feeling.

"It's all here," he rose to clean up the mess and left the stable to discard it and to wash his hands at the water pump. Rebecca leaned against the stable wall and watched mother and baby.

Sabrina looked down at her protruding belly, rubbing her hand over it and thought about the child growing within her. She ached for the child who would never know her father and for the father who would never hold his child. The next thing she knew, she was lying in bed with Jemima, Caroline and Hilda busily working about her.

"Just one more push and I believe the baby's head'll emerge," Jemima patted Sabrina's knees and Caroline and Hilda stood on either side of her helping her push. Sabrina bore down with all her might as the contraction increased in intensity. She screamed in pain and Jemima exclaimed, "Here it is, here's the head! It's got your dark hair, sweetie!"

Sabrina flopped back breathing deeply as the contraction passed and she had a moment of reprieve. As the next contraction mounted, she felt the urge to push and began to sit up, Caroline and Hilda supported her again as she bore down one more time, screaming as the shoulders emerged and the rest of the baby's body flowed effortlessly.

"You did it, Brina! It's a little girl!" Jemima held up the baby for Sabrina to see as Caroline rushed to put a blanket around the baby. Sabrina flopped back on her pillow and

inhaled deeply as tears of joy and accomplishment streamed
from her eyes.

"Here's your little girl, sweetie." Jemima placed a tightly
wrapped bundle in her arms. Only the baby's head with her
little chubby cheeks and black fuzzy hair emerged from the
white blanket. Love filled Sabrina's heart as a tear dripped
onto the baby's blanket.

"Becca, you all right?" Mitch crouched in front of her.
Rebecca snapped from her reverie to find Mitch wiping the
tears from her cheek with his thumb.

"Oh," she quickly moved her hands to her face to brush
away the remaining tears.

"What's wrong?" he asked.

"I just had another vision," she replied.

"What was it?" he sat down next to her as if he intended
to stay with her until she told him all about it.

"Sabrina had a baby girl," she hesitated. "And I think
I've solved the mystery ... I think Sabrina is my real mother."

Mitch's eyes lit with understanding as he watched her
dab at her tears with a handkerchief. "How do you feel about
that?"

"I – I don't know – different, I guess, like I'm not who I
always thought I was," she stared at the horse and the foal.

"You're still the same person, Becca. Nothin's changed
who you are inside," he reassured.

She suddenly rose to her feet and looked down at him,
"Until a few moments ago I thought I was Ethan and
Caroline Marchant's daughter and now I'm the illegitimate
child of his sister and her Union soldier lover. I was someone

respectable and decent and now I'm somethin' so shameful that people have to lie and keep secrets because of me."

Mitch stood and put his hands on her shoulders, "Listen to me now, Becca. You're still respectable and decent. You *are* Ethan and Caroline Marchant's daughter. They raised you to be who you are. They loved you and none o' the shame you're feelin' is your fault."

"But I'm a product of… of…"

He put a hand to her cheek, directing her to look at him, "You're the product of two people's love – two people who made a mistake in the timin' o' things but God blessed Ethan and Caroline through that mistake." Mitch pulled her to him enfolding her in his arms as she rested her head on his shoulder and put her arms around his waist. It felt so comforting to be held by him as if while her perception of herself and the family she'd known tossed on a billowing wave, this man stood before her as an anchor to keep her from sinking.

"Why did you decide to decline the marriage proposal, Becca?" he asked her for the third time.

She gazed into his gray-blue eyes and finally answered, "Because I trust myself when I'm with him." Then, she pulled her arms from around Mitch's waist and briskly left his side. Pausing at the stable door she turned back, "I need to speak with Grandma. I'll send Uncle Edmund out to see the foal." Mitch thrust his hands into his pockets as an understanding smile spread across his handsome face.

It was dark, but the moon and stars shone brightly when Rebecca entered the house. She passed Uncle Edmund on the stairs. "The Appaloosa had her foal. He's a beauty," she told him.

"Good," Edmund headed straight for the door and outside.

Rebecca tapped on Jemima's door, "Grandma, are you awake?"

"Yes, dear, come on in," Jemima answered. She still sat in her rocker sewing.

Rebecca sat down on the bed facing her grandmother.

"So how did it go?" Jemima put down her sewing and looked expectantly at Rebecca.

"We worked it out. Uncle Edmund told him I was engaged," Rebecca sighed. "Why would he do that?"

"I suppose he thought you were and he was tryin' to protect you," Jemima shrugged her shoulders.

"Why would he think I was engaged? I never told anyone that I planned to accept Mr. Phillips' proposal. I even gave him back the ring before I left," she explained.

"I don't know. Why don't you ask your uncle for yourself?"

"I suppose I could, but he sort o' makes me nervous," Rebecca admitted.

"Edmund's as harmless as a lamb, dear. Just ask him," Jemima reassured.

"Maybe I will later, but first I have a question for you," Rebecca's heart began to pound. While she assumed she knew the truth, she wouldn't know for sure until Jemima confirmed it. "Am I... Am I Sabrina and Grant's daughter?"

Jemima sighed, "You've had another vision then?"

"Yes, of Sabrina giving birth to a baby girl." She hesitated, "It was me wasn't it?"

"Yes, dear," Jemima closed her eyes and nodded. "Caroline wanted a baby so badly and they did hope to have their own children in addition to you, but they never could. You see now how blessed we've been because you were with us? You see now how God can make miracles from mistakes, treasure from tragedy and hope from hopelessness?"

"If my being born is such a miracle and a treasure then why did everyone feel such a need for secrecy and lies?" Rebecca dabbed at her tears angrily. "Why couldn't people just be truthful about it all? Why did I have to find out this way?"

"Now be realistic dear. Is this the kind of thing you tell a small child? Would you have understood? And even as a young woman, what would the knowledge of this done to your perception of yourself or of your natural parents? Ethan and Caroline wanted to protect you from all that."

"But they're gone now. Why did you keep it from me after I arrived here?"

"Because the last thing I knew from Ethan and Caroline was that you were never to know. That was their wish and I didn't feel it was my place to go against the wishes of the dead."

"So the dead took matters into their own hands," Rebecca felt goose bumps tingling across her arms and back.

"I suppose so. Perhaps God knew it was time for you to know. And although I'm sure it's painful for you to know the truth, don't you think this way was better?"

"To be haunted by waking dreams and night visions is better than someone just telling you truthfully? I don't know about that!" Rebecca shook her head in frustration.

"Think about it, Rebecca. You said for yourself earlier that you would have judged Sabrina harshly had you not lived her memories and shared her emotions. What if we had just told you this? How would you feel about Sabrina and Grant and even yourself had you only known the cold hard facts?"

Rebecca thought for a minute and muttered, "I see what you mean. Yes, I suppose this way is better." Rebecca nodded then suddenly stood, "Well, at least I'm free of it all now! No more dreams or visions!" Rebecca released a sigh of relief. "Now I just have to rediscover who I am." Rebecca flung her hands in the air.

"Oh, you're the same girl you've always been Rebecca, perhaps a little wiser and more compassionate," Jemima reassured.

"Then why do I feel like a foreigner in my own body? Every time I look in the mirror I'll think of Sabrina and the tragedy of it all."

"Now you know why Hilda drops plates," Jemima chuckled and rose to her feet embracing Rebecca, "You'll get used to it, dear. Give yourself some time to adjust."

"What happened to Sabrina, Grandma?" Rebecca finally asked the question that had been plaguing her mind. Inside she felt it, but wanted a straight answer.

"You don't know?" Jemima raised one eyebrow.

"I can guess, but I don't know for sure," she answered.

"Then perhaps you aren't free of those dreams yet, my dear," Jemima answered solemnly.

"Oh, Grandma, no! Please just tell me," Rebecca pleaded.

"Let's give it time to unfold," Jemima took up her sewing again, working intently. "Goodnight dear."

Rebecca sighed heavily. "Goodnight, Grandma," Rebecca kissed Jemima's cheek and left for her own bedroom.

Rebecca stood outside Edmund's oak study door, mustering the courage to knock. She'd had some time to sleep on what she would say to him. Finally, she raised her hand and knocked.

"Yes?" Edmund answered from within.

"It's Rebecca, Uncle Edmund, may I come in?" Rebecca answered.

"Yes."

Rebecca opened the door and peeked in, a wave of smoke hitting her face. "Are you busy?"

"Not too bad. Come on in," he motioned for her to enter and leaned back in his chair puffing on his cigar. "What can I do for you?"

"I just wanted to talk with you for a few minutes about somethin'. Grandma suggested it actually," she rubbed her hands together nervously.

"Go right ahead," he waited patiently.

"Well, it's come to my attention that you're aware of a recent marriage proposal I received, and I just wanted to let you know that I've decided to decline. I told him I'd think it over and I've decided it wouldn't be wise for me to accept. I'm writing him today to let him know."

"Really? He seems like a fine young man – good family, wealthy and well-respected."

"Well, yes, but… may I ask you how you're even aware of this proposal, Uncle? I never told anyone that I planned to accept it. I don't understand why you thought I had or even how you knew about it."

"Let's just say that the horse breedin' community is a small world," Edmund thumped his fingers on his desk.

"So who told you about it?" she pressed.

"I've had some dealings with the Phillips family in the past and I happened to be talking with young Stephen at a show and he mentioned it to me," Edmund answered.

"So Stephen told you that I had accepted his proposal?" Rebecca's heart began to pound and she gripped her fists tightly on the folds of her dress.

"Well, he told me that he'd asked for your hand and that your father had given his consent and that you were thinking about it. I just assumed you would accept such a generous proposal. I can't comprehend why anyone would refuse it," Edmund shrugged his shoulders and stared at her as if she must not have a brain between her ears.

Rebecca resisted the incredible urge she felt to argue and lowered her voice, "Mr. Phillips and I are friends, Uncle. Do you understand what I mean? It would be like… like marrying your cousin. There's just no feeling there." Rebecca realized how silly her explanation must seem to her emotionless uncle. "I suppose it's a girl thing." She waved her hand, "At any rate, I'm not marrying Stephen Phillips and I wanted you to know."

As she turned to leave the room, Edmund muttered, "Some people marry their cousins and are quite happy with them."

She hesitated in the doorway and turned her head toward him, "Well, I'm not one of them. I want more than that. Thank you for your time."

After she'd left his study, Edmund returned to his papers, shaking his head and muttering, "The apple sure doesn't fall far from the tree."

Later that afternoon, Edmund and Mitch loaded up two mares and a stallion to sell at an auction in Chattanooga. Rebecca would have loved to tag along, but didn't feel comfortable inviting herself, especially not after her recent interaction with her uncle.

When they arrived at the auction, Mitch unloaded the horses as Edmund went over to check in.

"Those are some fine lookin' animals you got there, Edmund," a deep voice bellowed from behind.

Edmund turned and extended his hand, "Dave Phillips, what are you doin' down here?"

"Lookin' for some new blood," he smiled as he shook Edmund's hand heartily.

"Perhaps we've got just what you're searchin' for," Edmund smiled.

"Well, I know you've got a filly out your way that my
boy's been hankerin' for," he chuckled. The smile evaporated
from Edmund's face. "How is your niece? She's good, I
hope?" Dave asked with concern.

Edmund looked around nervously to insure that Mitch
wasn't nearby. "My niece is… well, she's probably writin'
your son a letter as we speak."

"Really? He'll be glad to get that. He's received only one
from her since she's been gone and he said it was just a short
little thing."

Edmund sighed. He hated for a good business
relationship to be strained by personal entanglements, "I hate
to tell you this, Dave, but she's turnin' down his proposal.
Not got a brain in her head, I'm afraid." Edmund shook his
head disgustedly.

"What? Why?"

"Who knows what makes a female do anythin'?"
Edmund muttered.

"This is gonna kill Stephen," Dave winced. "Can't you
talk some sense into her?"

"You're talkin' to the wrong fella, Dave. I've never had a
lick a luck talkin' sense into a female," Edmund shook his
head.

"I could make it worth your while if ya did," Dave's
eyebrows rose in a plotting stare.

"What do ya have in mind?"

"Think about it, Edmund. If Stephen married your niece,
together we'd have my stock, yours *and* your brother's. We
could have the horse market sown up 'round here. Think o'

the prize winners we could get out o' the three farms. I think
we could do some amazin' business. Don't ya think?

Edmund stroked his chin, "Uh humm... I see whatcha
mean there. But she ain't gonna listen to me. But..." he
hesitated.

"What?"

"I do have an idea. Rebecca's one of those females driven
by what my brother would call sparks 'n' magic. No sparks,
no magic, no marriage. She's gotten herself confused since
she's been down here and that there horse trainer o' mine is
largely the cause of it." He nodded in Mitch's direction.

"Then get rid o' him," Dave stated flatly.

"Nope, can't do that. He's the best around. Irreplaceable.
But, if your Stephen came for a visit and brought along some
sparks 'n' magic of his own with his other fine qualities"

"Like affluence and position," Dave interjected.

"Right... I think standin' side by side, she'd choose the
better man," Edmund continued to rub his chin.

"I see what ya mean. She's just forgotten what a great
catch my Stephen is!" Dave added confidently.

"This way'd be better than sendin' Mitch away. She'd
just pine for 'im that way. Trust me, ain't nothin' worse than
a woman pinin' for a man she's lost. You'll never talk any
sense into her then. But if it's her own choice, then you've got
no ghosts to haunt the marriage."

"I thought you said you didn't understand women,
Edmund?" Dave chuckled.

"Well, I've had a little experience," he shrugged his
shoulders.

Jemima and Rebecca strolled into Mrs. Carrington's dress shop on Market Street. It was Rebecca's first trip into Chattanooga. Jemima felt it was time to clear Rebecca's head a bit and let her enjoy the sights and sounds of the city. She'd planned a small dinner evening in Rebecca's honor and invited all her friends and their families to attend.

"Pick any dress you'd like Rebecca," Jemima smiled.

"Oh, you don't need to buy anything for me. I'm just happy to be out and about and see the city," Rebecca smiled.

"I want to. Find somethin' that'll get ol' Mitch's heart ta pumpin' Saturday night,'" Jemima giggled.

"Grandma! I couldn't possibly!" Rebecca threw her hand to her bosom in surprise.

"Yes you could! Let's see here. I like this one," Jemima picked up a bright red dress with a heart shaped neck.

"Good grief, Grandma. Uncle Edmund *will* be callin' me a trollop in that one!" Rebecca rolled her eyes.

Jemima held it up to Rebecca, "Yep, that oughta get him to pop the question."

"Grandma!"

"I'm old, Rebecca. My only joy in life is teasin' ya and watchin' ya squirm," Jemima chuckled.

"Well, at least you're honest," Rebecca muttered. "Here, this one looks pretty," Rebecca picked up a modest cream colored dress with a small flowered print.

"I'm not buyin' you that! I brought you in here to get somethin' that would help you catch your man, not hide ya behind a flower sack!" Jemima rolled her eyes.

"Grandma, I never thought anyone could be worse than Aunt Miriam, but you are!" Rebecca shoved her fist soundly to her hip. "I really don't need a dress. I have plenty of nice dresses."

"Then, I'll just buy this one," Jemima grabbed the red dress and carried it to the counter.

"Grandma, no!" Rebecca whispered in embarrassment.

"I'd like to buy this dress for my granddaughter. May she use your dressin' room to try it on for size?" Jemima asked.

"Why certainly, Mrs. Marchant. Come along dear. That dress would look lovely against your beautiful skin and dark hair – an excellent choice." Mrs. Carrington started toward the dressing room.

"Grandma, I've never worn red in my life! My mama will roll over in her grave," Rebecca whispered as Jemima pushed Rebecca into the dressing room and shoved the dress into her hands.

"Try it on, Rebecca, or I'll tell Mitch he makes you weak in the knees," Jemima giggled.

"You wouldn't!"

"Try me!" Jemima's eyes gave her a stern warning.

"I'll need some help fastening this," Rebecca muttered.

Jemima entered the dressing room and helped Rebecca fasten the dress, "Oh, my, my! It's a perfect fit and you look absolutely stunning. Wear your hair like you did that day Hilda dropped the plate and Mitch won't know what hit 'im."

"Grandma, what makes you think I want Mitch to …to…"

"You think we're all blind, Rebecca? He'll make a fine husband for you. Besides bein' insanely handsome, he's a perfect one to carry back to help you run your daddy's farm. Edmund'll hate to see 'im go, but we'll muddle through somehow."

"You've got this all planned out, don't you?" Rebecca asked incredulously. "You probably had it all planned out before I even got here," she gasped.

"Honest I didn't, but once I saw you ridin' back over the hill with 'im that first day, I knew it," Jemima chuckled.

"You *are* a hopeless romantic, aren't you? Why don't you put some of that schemin' and plottin' to your own benefit and remarry?" Rebecca whispered.

"Oh, I'm too old for all that," Jemima shook her head.

"No, you're not. You still look so young and beautiful and you're full of energy. Why don't you invite a handsome widower to the party?" Rebecca thought she'd put the shoe on the other foot for a change. She slipped out of the dress and replaced her own, then stepped out of the dressing room and marched up to Mrs. Carrington. "Mrs. Carrington, do you know any handsome widowers we could invite to our dinner party on Saturday night? I think my Grandma needs a beau," Rebecca mustered every ounce of energy to proceed boldly without cracking a smile.

"Rebecca!" Jemima scolded in a whisper and looked around the dress shop hoping no one she knew overheard Rebecca's remark.

Mrs. Carrington answered, "Matter of fact, my brother Harrison is a widower. Poor thing lost his wife two years ago this winter. It's about time he remarried."

"Oh dear!" Jemima's eyes widened at Rebecca as her face flushed.

"Oh, let's give him our address and invite him to the party, shall we, Grandma?" Rebecca almost felt guilty for enjoying herself so much at her grandmother's expense. But she continued, "Here, Mrs. Carrington, do you have a paper and pen?"

"Rebecca, that's enough. I'm sorry to trouble you Mrs. Carrington. Let me pay for this dress and we'll be on our way," Jemima tugged at Rebecca's arm as Mrs. Carrington handed Rebecca a paper and writing utensil.

Jemima's teasing of Rebecca hadn't gone unnoticed by Mrs. Carrington and she enjoyed the opportunity to help the young women in her game of revenge, "Actually, Mrs. Marchant, I believe you and my brother would hit it off nicely. I'll give him your invitation. I'm sure he'd attend. Just right down when and where there, Miss Rebecca."

"This is insane, Rebecca!" Jemima whispered in Rebecca's ear as she thrust some money into Mrs. Carrington's hand and then tugged on Rebecca's arm.

"Now you know how it feels! Oh, and let's find you a dress too now that you have a suitor for the evening." Rebecca scurried toward a rack of dresses and began thumbing through them. "Oh, this one would look lovely on you, Grandma!" She grabbed a beautiful navy blue dress and hurried to hold it up in front of Jemima."

Jemima stared at her incredulously, "All right, Rebecca, you've made your point. Enough of that now."

"We've got this far, Grandma. I'll wear that red dress *and* arrange my hair like Sabrina's Saturday night, if you'll buy this one and wear it for Mrs. Carrington's brother."

Jemima grabbed the dress, "You've got a deal."

Chapter 7

Rebecca stood in front of the mirror in her petticoats and corset fiddling with her hair when she heard a knock at her door.

"Yes?" Rebecca called.

"It's me, Grandma, may I come in?"

"Sure," Rebecca answered.

Jemima entered the room wearing her new blue dress with her hair swept up and elegantly arranged.

"Oh, Grandma, you look gorgeous!" Rebecca gasped and Jemima shut the door.

"Thank you, dear," Jemima smiled. "And you're even more beautiful than your mother."

"Hardly," Rebecca sighed.

"Oh yes, you have Grant's eyes. They're Sabrina's color, but the shape of 'em's Grant's. He had such striking eyes, ya know."

"Yes, I do know," Rebecca smiled.

"I brought you somethin' I found," Jemima handed Rebecca a small tin type.

Rebecca gasped, "It's them!" She felt a chill run along her shoulders and up to her neck as she gazed at the picture of

Grant in his uniform with Sabrina at his side. "She *does* look just like me!"

"Remarkable isn't?" Rebecca nodded and Jemima continued, "I found it in an old hatbox of Sabrina's that I've kept for you all these years. There are a few more things you'll find interestin' in it, but you'll need time to look through it all. So you can do that in the morning."

"Oh you *do* just love to torment me don't you? You wait until right before this dinner party and then tell me I've got a box of memories – knowing I can't look through it until tomorrow." Rebecca turned back to the photograph. "It's so odd, I look at this and I know them! It's so amazing, don't you think, that I *know* them?"

"It's a gift – a priceless gift you've been given," Jemima whispered as she stood next to her looking at the photograph. As Rebecca ran her fingers gently across the tin type, Jemima went to Rebecca's closet and pulled out the red dress and held it up next to Rebecca.

"Oh must I really, Grandma? I hoped you'd let me off the hook," Rebecca whined.

"Not now that Mr. Harrison Thurman has officially accepted his invitation. I don't even know anything about the man!" Jemima shoved the dress at Rebecca who set the photograph on her dresser. "So you, my dear, are keepin' your end o' this bargain! At least you've got a young buck waitin' on you. I could be stuck with an ugly ol' toad all evenin'!"

"Oh, I'm sure he's not an ugly old toad, Grandma! And if you don't like him, make Uncle Edmund entertain 'im," Rebecca chuckled. "But you've pretty much cooked my goose with this dress. I'm gonna look like a woman desperate for attention! It's embarrasin'!"

"No you won't, Rebecca. You'll look like an elegant beauty – just like your mama... both of 'em," Jemima winked and held up the dress for Rebecca to insert her arms.

Rebecca felt a wave of nervous jitters in her stomach as she stared at herself in the mirror – her hair swept up exposing her long neck in the elegant heart-shaped bodice which accentuated her feminine shape and tiny waist. Jemima stood behind her fastening the dress.

Jemima joined Rebecca in gazing at her reflection in the mirror. "Maybe this wasn't such a good idea after all," Jemima muttered.

"What?" Rebecca looked at her grandmother's serious reflection.

"We might be playin' with fire here. I think you may be too temptin' for a man to resist," Jemima winked. "No runnin' off to be by yourselves tonight," Jemima warned.

"Yes, ma'am," a strange flutter stirred within Rebecca as she slipped her gloves on her hands and followed Jemima out of her room and down the stairs.

Soon guests began arriving and with each knock, Rebecca held her breath in anticipation of Mitch's arrival. Jemima proudly introduced each guest to her granddaughter, many of whom knew Sabrina and gasped at the uncanny resemblance.

A group of people arrived simultaneously and Rebecca spied Mitch head and shoulders above the rest as he made his way into the house. Suddenly self-conscious, she blushed and showed an unusual interest in a little old lady who entered the room – anything to postpone the eventual encounter with him. As the lady moved on into the great room, Rebecca looked up to discover Mitch standing directly in front of her, his broad shoulders clad in a handsome suit. He gallantly took her gloved hand in his and kissed it then leaned over and whispered into her ear, "You're incredible, Becca." The warmth of his breath on her neck sent her heart palpitating and goose bumps prickling up her flesh culminating in a rosy heated blush at her cheeks. "Are you sure Hilda will have enough plates left for all these people?" his eyes twinkled as he extended his arm. She placed her hand on his arm and he led her into the dining room.

As Mitch pulled out Rebecca's chair for her, Rebecca noticed a tall, handsome gray-haired gentleman with twinkling green eyes pulling out a chair for her grandmother. Rebecca smiled at Jemima whose eyes widened. For Rebecca, the look on her grandmother's face at that moment was worth any embarrassment Rebecca felt at wearing the alluring red dress. Rebecca chuckled a little to herself and Mitch leaned over, placing his hand on her arm, "What's so funny?"

"My grandmother's blind date," she whispered in his ear and lingered momentarily inhaling his masculine scent of leather and witch hazel.

"She has a suitor?" Mitch's eyebrows rose as he glanced over at Jemima who now sat next to the dashing Harrison Thurman.

"Mmmm hmmm," Rebecca nodded.

"Well, this should prove interesting," he whispered.

163

Mitch's eyes rarely left Rebecca throughout dinner. She was so nervous that she could barely eat and did more nervous fiddling with her food than anything.

As dinner concluded, Mitch extended his arm to lead Rebecca into the great room where a small band began to play.

"Did you and your grandmother eat before everyone arrived? Neither one of you seem to have much of an appetite tonight," Mitch remarked.

"I guess we're both just a little nervous," Rebecca answered. "I for one always get a little flustered around so many people I don't know."

"Oh, is that it? I've never seen Mrs. Marchant flustered in my entire life – no matter how large the crowd, but tonight, she looks positively unnerved," he chuckled.

"Poor, Grandma," Rebecca grinned. "I sort of set her up."

"You did? Well, she doesn't look any worse for the wear," he nodded in Jemima's direction as Mr. Thurman took her in his arms to waltz. "Perhaps we should join them so your grandmother doesn't feel uncomfortable. May I have this dance, my lady?" he bowed exaggeratedly. She accepted his extended hand and Mitch took Rebecca in his arms.

Throughout the dance, she tried not to think about the way he made her feel inside and searched for anything to talk about that would divert her attention from the strength of his arms, his engaging smile and the twinkle in his gray blue eyes.

"Grandma found a picture of Sabrina and Grant. She showed it to me just before dinner. She says there's a whole hatbox full of memories that she'll give me tomorrow," she rattled nervously.

"Bet you'd rather be in your room rummaging through that than down here wastin' time dancin' with a stable hand," he teased.

"Not really," she smiled. "But would you care to see the picture sometime?"

"I'd be very curious to see it. Matter of fact, I'd like to see what treasures you find in that hatbox."

"Why don't you stop in tomorrow morning and we'll go through it together," she invited and then realized that would mean spending time alone with him – something that made her more nervous with each encounter.

"That sounds fun," he smiled and adjusted his hand at her back to pull her a little closer. When the song ended, Mitch felt a tap at his back and saw Rebecca's mouth drop wide open.

"What is it, Becca?" he asked.

"Stephen, what are you doin' here?" the color drained from her face.

Mitch still held her hand in his as he stepped back and his stormy eyes went from Rebecca to Stephen and back.

"Your uncle invited me, Rebecca. You look absolutely stunning tonight, my dear," he took her free hand in his and kissed it. "Sir, would you mind terribly if I danced with my fiancé?" Stephen gave Mitch a cold stare.

Taken by surprise, Mitch reluctantly released Rebecca's hand and allowed Stephen to dance with her. Mitch stepped back and watched angrily as Stephen pulled Rebecca into his arms and waltzed with her in a familiar manner. Rebecca tried to pull herself away to form a greater distance between them, but Stephen tugged her closer.

"Didn't - didn't you receive my letter?" she stammered.

"What letter would that be, my dear?" he affected ignorance. "You've barely written me since you've been gone."

"I wrote you a couple weeks ago that I've decided to decline your proposal," she blurted out.

"You did? Why ever would you do such a thing, Rebecca?"

"Mr. Phillips, I'm terribly sorry that you didn't receive the letter, and I'm even sorrier that my uncle has no regard for my wishes. I value our friendship, but I simply don't feel that we're compatible for … for marriage."

"How can we not be compatible, Rebecca? We have everything in common. You've just forgotten that."

"I haven't forgotten anything." She lowered her voice to a whisper, "I'm sorry, but I just don't feel that way about you."

"Give me a chance, Rebecca, and I can make you feel that way about me," he whispered in her ear.

"I'm sorry, Stephen, I'm really sorry to hurt you," she shook her head. "But it's just not meant to be between us."

"We make what's meant to be, Rebecca!" he suddenly became angry, but his voice was constrained to a low whisper. "Is it because of him?" he nodded in Mitch's direction.

Noting the tension rising between the dancing couple, Mitch tapped on Stephen's shoulder, "Excuse me." Stephen started to protest when Jemima appeared and grabbed Stephen's hand.

"Mr. Phillips!" so good to see you again. I haven't seen you since you were a little boy! Would you dance with an old friend of the family?" she exuded and tugged Stephen until he began to waltz with her.

Mitch laced his hand through Rebecca's fingers and guided her out onto the veranda. He looked around to find a couple standing on the porch talking.

"Let's go for a walk," he started toward the steps."

"Oh, we better not venture off," she shook her head.

"Just a short walk. We need to talk," he stepped down from the veranda gripping her hand tightly so she would follow.

"Is that him?" he asked.

"Yes, I have no idea what Uncle Edmund is up to inviting him. I told him that I had no intention of marrying him and I even sent Stephen a letter notifying him of my decision. He *claims* he never received it."

"So you didn't invite him?" Mitch asked.

"Of course not!" Rebecca stared into Mitch's relieved eyes and he took her arm.

They walked arm-in-arm for several minutes until they arrived at the corral which held the Appaloosa and her foal. Rebecca placed her hands on the fence and watched the foal and its mother by the light of the full moon. She could feel the warmth emanating from Mitch's broad shoulders as he stood comfortingly behind her blocking the chilly evening breeze. Rebecca's heart raced and she held her breath as she felt Mitch's gentle caress on the nape of her neck. She jumped slightly in exhilaration as his hand slid to her shoulder and his heated breath hovered above the flesh of her neck as he allowed his mustache to bristle along her skin where his hand had been moments before. His hands slipped to her sides and then his arms encircled her waist as he placed lingering kisses on her neck, his body warm against her back.

Her heart hammering within her, a wave of uncontrollable fear accompanied the thrill she felt at his touch. The feelings which stirred within her were too intense, too familiar, yet she'd never experienced them in reality until that moment. She spun around, placing her hand firmly to his chest. "Mitch, I think we need to go back."

He put a hand gently to her throat, caressing the softness of her long slender neck with his thumb. "Relax, Becca," he softly kissed the corners of her mouth.

"I can't," she put her hands to his chest as if to hold him at bay, but not forcefully enough for him to interpret it as instruction to cease.

The next thing she knew, his mouth was warm and confidently on hers, but she still wouldn't engage in his kiss. Her heart screamed that she should lose herself in his kisses, but she felt too terrified that the fire burning within her heart would consume her completely if she allowed it to roam free of its bonds.

Sensing her reservation, Mitch held her face in his hands, searched her eyes and whispered, "Becca, let them go. We're not Sabrina and Grant. It's just you and me. We're not gonna make their mistakes."

"How do you know that?" she whispered.

"Because I won't let it happen," he whispered and his mustache brushing across her neck below her ear sent a warm shiver throughout her body and she clenched her fists clutching tightly to the fabric of her dress.

"Leave them behind and be here with me tonight," he whispered as he pried her fists open and tugged the gloves from her hands. Mitch kissed her palms and placed them around his neck.

"Please Mitch…"

"Becca, if you can't allow yourself to be here with me, you may as well be with him," his eyes pointed toward Stephen Phillips who stood on the veranda watching from a distance with his chest rising and falling in controlled anger.

"I don't want him and you know it!" Rebecca insisted breathlessly.

"Prove it to 'im," Mitch dared, staring at her with his penetrating gray blue eyes. "Prove it to me."

Her heart drumming in her ears, Rebecca allowed her fingers to roam through his thick blond locks and to caress the softness of the back of his neck.

"Prove it, Becca," Mitch repeated and Rebecca pulled his mouth to hers and kissed his bottom lip tenderly. Mitch stood there, letting her kiss him, making her prove the point that it was *she* who was choosing *him*.

It took every ounce of courage that Rebecca could muster to place lingering kisses on his lips without him returning her affections and the seconds seemed like hours as she wondered how long he would wait before he finally returned her kisses. Then suddenly without warning, the fire burning within her heart escaped its bonds and filled her entire being as he fully engaged himself in her embrace, returning her

affections in a passionate blaze that rivaled anything
Rebecca could dream or imagine.

Reluctantly and breathlessly, she put her hands to either
side of his face and sighed, "Have I proven my point?"

"Yes, I'd say you have," Mitch leaned his forehead to
hers as he took a deep breath and exhaled, "I guess we
should go back now." Pulling her gloves from his pocket, he
handed them to her and she slipped them back on. She slid
her arm through his and he put his free hand on hers,
caressing it gently as he led her back to the house. Seeing
them approach, Stephen stepped inside the house to seek out
his father.

"Father, let's go," Stephen's face was nearly as red as his
hair.

"We just got here. Why should we leave?" Dave
shrugged his shoulders and turned back to continue his
conversation with Edmund.

"Well, I'm leavin'," he started for the door and Dave
grabbed his arm. "Edmund, do you have somewhere that I
can have a moment alone with my son?"

"You can use my study," Edmund motioned for the two
to follow him. Edmund held the door open for them and
turned to leave.

"No, Edmund, please stay here. I think I may need your
help to talk some sense into my boy," Dave motioned for
Edmund to enter the room. Reluctantly Edmund stepped in
and shut the door behind them.

"So what's goin' on, Stephen?" Dave prodded.

"I, uh…" he looked toward Edmund hesitantly.

"It's all right; you can speak in front of Mr. Marchant. He's an ally here," Dave insisted.

"It's over between Miss Marchant and myself, and I'd just like to leave quietly, Father," Stephen explained.

"What do you mean it's over? We barely got here," consternation grew more evident on Dave's face.

"It doesn't take long to see when a woman's in love with someone else. I'd be a fool to hang around in hopes of persuading her any differently," hurt flickered across Stephen's face and he looked as if he would bolt from the room that very instant.

Dave grabbed his son's shoulders, "Now look here, boy, you haven't even tried yet. Put on the ol' charm. Edmund here says his niece goes for sparks 'n' magic. Give her some sparks 'n' magic."

"Dad, I just saw her gettin' plenty o' sparks 'n' magic from somebody else and I care too much for her to make a fool o' myself in her eyes," Stephen grew more resolute.

"Edmund, help me out here. Talk some sense into this boy," Dave turned to Edmund expecting an ally.

"Dave, I think you've got a sharp boy there. You can't turn a woman's head in such cases – at least not a woman like my niece. If she's anythin' like her mother, she'll listen to her heart over her head til her dyin' breath."

"What would it take for me to buy Garrison off o' ya?" Dave offered.

"What?" Stephen's voice rose in rebuke. "Dad!"

"It won't do you a lick o' good to try to buy 'im off, Dave. I've known that boy since he was knee high to a frog and he can't be bought, even if I fired him and sent him away, he'd never leave Rebecca's side. Even if he did go away, it wouldn't make Rebecca give her heart to Stephen."

Dave took a step toward Edmund, "What makes you so all-fired certain? You've barely been around the girl but for the last month. How can you predict what she'll do?"

"Because I knew her mother and this girl's her spittin' image in almost every sense of the word. Her mother wouldn't listen to reason once her heart started flutterin' and neither will her daughter. You're just wastin' your time. There's other ways we can do business here. Keep Mitch and Rebecca as friends, and we'll all be able to do business with 'em once they start runnin' Ethan's ranch.

"Ugggh," Dave growled and ran his fingers through his hair.

"It's the right thing to do, Dad. Let's just leave 'em be," Stephen put his arm on his father's shoulder.

"I still think you're givin' up too easy, Stephen," Dave shook his head.

"If you saw what I just saw, you wouldn't be sayin' that," Stephen shook his head.

"Edmund, we still need to talk over the price o' that Appaloosa and then we can be goin.'"

"Thank you for invitin' me, Mrs. Marchant. You're every bit as lovely as my sister described," Harrison Thurman bent his grey head forward to kiss Jemima's hand and his green eyes locked into Jemima's brown ones. Rebecca sat at the top of the stairs noting the blush in Jemima's cheeks as her suitor

bid her farewell. After Harrison left, Jemima slowly climbed
the stairs lost in thought until she came to Rebecca's knees
which were directly in front of her.

"Oh, Rebecca, I didn't see you there," Jemima stopped
abruptly.

"That's because you only have eyes for the dashing Mr.
Thurman," Rebecca chuckled.

"My teasin's comin' back to haunt me now isn't it?"
Jemima put her hand to her hip and waited for Rebecca to
move. Rebecca stood and started up the stairs.

Once Rebecca reached the top she turned to face Jemima.
"So are you gonna see him again?"

"Well of course. You think I'd let a catch like that pass
me by?" Jemima released a youthful giggle.

"Grandma! Then you really like him?" Rebecca smiled.

"Yes, I do. He's a nice man," Jemima nodded and started
for her bedroom.

"I'm glad!" Rebecca's smile spread from ear to ear.

"I just wish your mama was here to see you tonight,
Rebecca," Jemima motioned for Rebecca to follow her into her
bedroom.

"Which mama?" Rebecca asked.

"Both of 'em, but I was thinkin' particularly of Sabrina.
She was always fond of Mitch as a lad. To think you two are
endin' up together!" Jemima shook her head with the irony of
it.

"What makes you think we're endin' up together?"
Rebecca began her usual protest but Jemima held up her
hand to stop her.

"Don't be pretendin' like there's nothin' happenin' between you two. Stephen Phillips wasn't the only one who caught an eyeful with that moment out by the corral." Jemima's eyebrows rose accusatorily.

Rebecca's cheeks flushed crimson as she threw her hands over her face, "Oh no!" Rebecca lowered her hands enough to peek through her fingers. "You were watchin' that?"

"Uh huh," Jemima nodded.

"Did anyone else see? How mortifying!"

"Pretty much just me and Mr. Phillips – maybe a couple other folks."

Rebecca flopped down on Jemima's bed and put her arms over her head, "Oh I think I'm gonna be sick!"

"Embarrasin' as it may be, it did do the trick where Mr. Phillips' concerned. He left shortly after that. Don't think he'll be botherin' you anymore."

"Oh, I can't believe this!" Rebecca felt like crawling in a hole and hiding for a year.

"As much as you go on, I must admit I was surprised to see you throw yourself at a man like that, Rebecca," Jemima teased.

"I did not *throw* myself at him!" Rebecca began her defense.

Jemima's eyebrows rose in disbelief.

"Oh!" Rebecca whined exasperatedly. "I was just tryin' to prove a point."

"Well you proved it all right!" Jemima chuckled.

"I'm wastin' my time tryin' to explain this to you," Rebecca huffed and she headed for the door. "Good night Grandma!"

"Good night, dear. I'm glad you had such a good time," Jemima winked and Rebecca closed the door as she left the room.

Edmund entered the stable to find Mitch saddling his horse to leave. "Hello there Mitch, I'm glad I caught you before you left tonight."

Mitch braced himself. He was still aggravated that Edmund had invited Stephen Phillips to the dinner party when he knew that Rebecca didn't care for him and had rejected his proposal.

"How can I help you, Sir?" Mitch lifted his head toward Edmund, forcing himself to be amicable.

"You evidently disobeyed my last instructions regarding my niece so I'd like to know what your intentions are toward her?"

Mitch stared at him, unsure how to answer.

"I mean, whatever Stephen Phillips saw between you and Rebecca tonight made him give up on all hopes of marryin' her. That marriage would've meant a lot to us all – monetarily speakin' anyway. So since Rebecca's thrown that away for your sake, I want to know what your intentions are."

Mitch took a deep breath.

Rebecca stood at her bedroom window and noticed the lantern burning in the stable. Edmund stood with his hands on his hips conversing with Mitch. The two men seemed to be carrying on an in depth discussion and finally Edmund reached out his hand to shake Mitch's and turned back toward the house, after which Mitch mounted his horse and rode away.

Rebecca, Jemima and Edmund sat down to breakfast in silence. Rebecca still felt animosity toward her uncle for inviting Stephen to the party. Finally she blurted out, "Uncle Edmund, why did you invite Stephen Phillips to the party last night when you knew I had rejected his proposal? It was incredibly embarrassing!"

"We were talkin' business," Edmund put a fork full of eggs in his mouth.

"Business? That's all?" Rebecca asked incredulously.

"It was all business, Rebecca – nothin' personal, just business," Edmund nodded.

"Oh," she looked down at her plate and stabbed at her sausage link with her fork.

"It didn't hurt anythin' for him to be here anyway, you know. It actually helped you. It was somethin' he needed to see to understand," Edmund began to explain.

"Are you sayin' you invited him here to see that I'm… that I've moved on?" she set her fork down and stared in disbelief that her uncle had actually been trying to help her.

"I told Dave that you can't reason with a woman who's feelin' sparks 'n' magic, but he wouldn't believe me, so I thought it would be best to show Stephen," Edmund shrugged.

"And you did show him didn't you, dear?" Jemima winked at Rebecca who shot her grandmother a wide-eyed horrified stare.

Edmund turned to Jemima, "Not sure what happened last night exactly, but yes, I believe she did."

"I'm sorry. I'm really not that hungry. May I be excused?" Rebecca asked as she scooted her chair back.

"Oh, I didn't mean to upset you with my teasin', dear. Please stay and finish your breakfast," Jemima apologized.

"I'm kind of anxious to take a look at Sabrina's things. Can you please tell me where the box is so I can go get it?" Rebecca asked.

"Oh that's right," Jemima smiled.

"I still can't get over the fact that Papa had a sister and he never even told me about her," Rebecca shook her head as she rose from her seat.

"A sister?" Edmund gave Rebecca a puzzled gaze. "What're you talkin' about?"

"Sabrina, your sister - didn't Grandma tell you I know all about her and Grant?"

Edmund looked toward Jemima, "Yes, she told me, but Sabrina isn't my *sister*."

"She isn't?" Rebecca looked at Edmund and then to Jemima.

"No, she's my cousin Martha's daughter. She came to live with us when her parents died. Sabrina was what ..."

Jemima looked to Edmund, "fourteen maybe when she came to live with us?"

"Yeah, it was the summer I turned twenty," Edmund nodded.

"You thought Sabrina was my daughter this whole time?" Jemima asked.

"Well, Sabrina and I look so much like you. Mitch and I just assumed..." Rebecca began. "So I'm really not even your granddaughter at all?" Rebecca stared at Jemima and felt as if someone had just punched her in the stomach.

"Oh, yes you are, dear! You've always been and always will be my granddaughter," Jemima rose from her seat and embraced Rebecca.

"So how are we related again?" Rebecca stared at Jemima still trying to absorb the latest jolt.

"My uncle Jasper had a daughter named Martha. Sabrina is her daughter. Martha and her husband Henry died from the influenza and Sabrina came to live with us."

A knock at the front door interrupted Rebecca's concentration. Jefferson opened the door and Rebecca turned to see Mitch step inside. He entered the living room and looked toward where Jemima and Rebecca stood in the dining room. "We still have a date this mornin', Becca?"

"Oh yes, I was just tellin' Grandma that I wanted to look through Sabrina's things. I'm glad you're here." Rebecca turned back toward Jemima, "Mitch wants to look through the box too. He remembers Sabrina, you know."

"I was just tellin' Rebecca last night how fond Sabrina always was of you as a boy," Jemima smiled.

"She was a lot of fun. I remember missin' her when she was gone," Mitch took Rebecca's hand. When Rebecca noted the unspoken communication that passed between Edmund and Mitch, she wondered what they had discussed out in the stable the night before.

"Mitch, Edmund and I were just tellin' Rebecca that Sabrina isn't my daughter. She's my cousin Martha's daughter. She came to live with us when her parents died when she was fourteen."

"Really? She wasn't your sister, Sir?" Mitch looked at Edmund. "I could have sworn she was!"

"No, she's definitely *not* my sister," Edmund muttered. Mitch turned to see how Rebecca was taking the news.

"Grandma, where's the hatbox, I'd really like to look through it now," Rebecca forced a smile.

Jemima started toward the door. "I'll have to go get it for you. I've got it put away upstairs."

As Jemima started up the stairs, Mitch called to her, "Becca and I'll be outside on the porch."

"All right, I'll just be a few minutes," Jemima answered.

"Are you all right?" he whispered once they stepped outside and he shut the door. She didn't answer but looked down at her feet. He put one hand to her waist and the other cupped the side of her face, forcing her to look at him. A tear shimmered in the corner of her eye.

"You're upset aren't you?"

"It seems like every day, a piece of who I am – the floor I'm standing on – crumbles away leaving me nowhere to stand anymore – until I'm just out here all by myself hangin' by a limb in mid air." She brushed at the tear that escaped from the corner of her eye.

Mitch grabbed Rebecca's hand and led her to a rocking chair. He backed into the rocker, sitting down in it, pulling her onto his lap.

"Mitch!" she gasped and struggled to stand up.

"No, sit here for a minute and let me tell you somethin'."

"What?" she brushed angrily at the tear that trickled down her cheek.

"Becca, most of us are surrounded by folks who're stuck with us. They have to love us 'cause we were born into their families and they've got no choice in the matter. But you, Becca, are surrounded by people who love you by choice. Jemima *chose* to take Sabrina into her home. Ethan and Caroline *chose* to be your parents. Jemima *chose* to be your Grandma and Edmund *chose* to be your uncle. They all love you by choice. That says a lot about you, Becca. You're loveable," he winked.

Rebecca blushed. He was just too sweet and thoughtful to resist. Sitting there on his lap, she felt entirely too tempted to throw her arms around his neck and kiss him then and there.

"You're not alone. You have all of us who love you here with you holdin' you up – just like I'm sittin' here holdin' you right now."

She put her arm on his shoulder and kissed his check, "Thank you, Mitch. You always know what to say to make me feel better." She started to rise and he pulled her back onto his lap.

"Just a sec, I've got one more thing to say,"

"Say it fast, 'cause if Grandma comes out here and finds us in this position, she'll be demandin' that you choose me too," she chuckled.

"Well, that's just what I wanted to talk with ya about, Becca. I'm kind o' hopin' that that kiss you gave me last night means you've chosen me cause if you'll have me, I'd consider myself blessed to wake up every mornin' to your beautiful face."

"What?" she whispered unable to believe what he had said. Her pulse raced and she had to make herself close her mouth which had flown open in surprise.

"I'm sayin' I love you, Becca. I've loved you since the first day I met you out by the creek. If you're searchin' for solid ground to stand on, darlin', stand by me. Will you be my bride?"

Rebecca encircled his neck with her arms, "Yes! Yes, I'll marry you!" She embraced him feeling his cheek against hers as she spoke into his ear, "I think I've loved you since that day in the cabin at Snodgrass Hill."

"You mean when you flung yourself at me?" he chuckled.

"Yes," she smiled as she gazed into his twinkling eyes, put her hand on his cheek and leaned forward placing joyous kisses on his lips.

Chapter 8

$\mathscr{T}$he front door opened and Jemima stepped quickly out onto the front porch and laid the hatbox next to the rocker. Rebecca nervously jumped from Mitch's lap and started for the door peeking her head in. Mitch rose from the rocker and stood looking toward the door in anticipation.

"Grandma, I'm sorry! Did you want to look through this with us?"

"That's all right dear, you two go right ahead. I know what's there." Jemima winked and walked into the living room.

"Thank you!" Rebecca smiled, closed the door and lifted the box from the porch.

"I guess we'll have some explaining to do later," Mitch chuckled.

"Yes, I'd say so," Rebecca rolled her eyes nervously. Her heart was still pounding from being caught in Mitch's lap.

Rebecca crossed to the porch steps and sat down on the porch with her feet on the steps. She tapped the floor next to her and motioned for Mitch to join her there. He sat next to her and Rebecca carefully untied the blue ribbons from around the flowered hatbox. Pulling the pink tissue from the top, she retrieved a photograph of Grant in his military uniform. Rebecca smiled and handed the photograph to Mitch.

"Well, there's your handsome father."

"He doesn't feel like my father," Rebecca mumbled.

"No, I suspect he wouldn't," Mitch remarked as he placed the picture on his lap.

"Here's the photograph Grandma showed me last night. She must've put it back in here." Rebecca held it so that Mitch could look at it too.

"Yep, that's the Sabrina I remember. See how much you look like her!" he turned to smile at her.

"It is uncanny, isn't it?" she marveled.

"Look!" Rebecca exclaimed. She handed Mitch a photograph of Sabrina holding a small baby. "This is our house in Kentucky! And I look maybe three months old there with Sabrina. I had assumed she died immediately after I was born, but it doesn't look like it."

"You were a cute little baby." Mitch smiled at the photograph. Finally he asked, "What makes you think Sabrina's dead? Did someone tell you she was?"

Rebecca searched her memory, "No, I don't believe anyone ever told me she was. I just assumed."

"Kind of how we assumed she was Edmund's sister?" Mitch's eyebrows rose.

"Yes, kind of like that. Maybe she's *not* dead after all," Rebecca turned back to the box and pulled out a Union cap. Inside it laid a braided locket of brown hair tied with a navy blue ribbon. Rebecca gently caressed the lock of hair and turned the hat over to inspect it.

"It's Grant's," she handed it to Mitch and put her hands to her cheeks and brushed the tears away as Mitch put his arm around her, embracing her shoulders.

Removing some more tissue, she lifted a small bundle of letters tied up with a red ribbon.

"Love letters from Grant," she whispered and reverently put them on the stack that was forming on Mitch's lap.

"You're not gonna read 'em?"

"Oh no, I better not. What if she *is* still alive? It wouldn't be proper to read them," Rebecca shook her head.

"But they might give you more insight into her life or where she is now," Mitch suggested and began thumbing through the envelopes.

"No, Mitch! We shouldn't invade her privacy," Rebecca insisted.

"We're already invadin' it by lookin' through her things. What's the difference?"

Rebecca darted an irritated look.

"Let's just read the outside of 'em and make sure they were all written before you were born," Mitch slipped the ribbon off the stack and looked at the return addresses. "Here's one from Caroline and Ethan." He lifted the flap on the envelope and started to pull the letter from inside.

"No Mitch, it's private," Rebecca warned.

"This isn't a love letter. It may give us some insight into what happened after your birth. Nobody's gonna mind. After all Jemima gave us the hatbox," he opened the letter and began to read.

Rebecca's Reveries

October 15, 1865

Dear Sabrina,

These are happy days for Ethan and myself. We are enjoying little Becca so much! She's growing like a weed and is sitting up now. She giggles delightedly when Ethan tickles her tummy. We wish you could see her and hope that you will come for a visit again soon. Every day we thank God for your unselfishness in allowing us to raise your little angel. She's a joy beyond compare and she reminds us so much of you that we long to see you again. Please do visit when you can.

With our love,

Ethan and Caroline

"Sounds like Sabrina gave you to Ethan and Caroline to raise. Would've been hard for her to raise a baby alone, I'd imagine," Mitch studied Rebecca's reaction to see how she was taking the revelation.

"Are there any more like that," Rebecca asked solemnly.

"Let's see," Mitch thumbed through the letters and opened an envelope. "Here's another one from Ethan and Caroline. This one's a little earlier than the last one." He handed it to her for her to read.

August 12, 1865

Dear Sabrina,

Ethan and I hope this letter finds you well and that you're fully recovered from the birth. We had a good trip back home and the baby traveled well. We have missed you and so has the baby. We know it was such a sacrifice for you to give her up, and we will do our best to show her the love that she would have received from you and Grant. She's smiling so much now. We will write often and send pictures when we can.

With our love,

Ethan and Caroline

Rebecca folded the letter and handed it back to Mitch to put with the others.

"Sounds like you were born here at Soquili and that Caroline and Ethan took you to Kentucky with them," he observed. He pulled another one out and handed it to her. She opened it carefully and began to read.

January 23, 1866

Dear Sabrina,

We're sorry to hear that you'll be leaving Soquili, but understand why you feel the need to go. We're glad that you agree with us about keeping things from little Rebecca until she's old enough to understand. We think you're right that it would only serve to confuse her. We will continue to write to you in Nashville and hope that the position works out satisfactorily for you there.

With love,

Ethan and Caroline

"Nashville – so she moved to Nashville. Are there anymore?" she asked as she folded the letter up and handed it to him.

"No, everything else looks like letters from Grant," Mitch muttered. He slipped the ribbon back around the bundle and put it inside of Grant's hat. Rebecca removed another layer of tissue paper and her hands began to tremble as she lifted an envelope from inside.

"It's an envelope addressed to me," Rebecca whispered.

She set it on her lap and traced her fingers over the inscription of her name. When she didn't open the envelope Mitch spoke, "Would you rather be alone to read it? I can leave."

"Oh no, no stay with me please," she whispered and squeezed his hand momentarily. Her heart began to pound and she put her hand to her bosom. "I don't know why I'm so nervous."

"It's only natural, I'd imagine. It's almost like a letter from beyond or somethin'," Mitch muttered.

"Yes, it's sort of eerie isn't it… to find a letter addressed to me – written years before I'd ever even read it?" she wiped the nervous perspiration from her hands onto her skirt.

"You want me to read it?" he offered.

"That's all right. I'll do it," she carefully opened the envelope and removed its contents. "It's dated the first of February 1866. I would've only been about … let's see… about eight months old." Rebecca read the letter aloud to Mitch.

Dear Rebecca,

You are only a small baby as I write this letter, but I anticipate that you will be a beautiful young woman by the time you read it. I have asked Ethan and Caroline to explain about me when you are old enough to understand and have asked Cousin Jemima to give this letter to you before you wed.

I hope and pray every day that you have found happiness throughout your life. You are a cherished treasure which I never wished to release, but I feel it is important that you have the opportunity to be raised in a home with a mother and a father who love you dearly and who love each other devotedly. This is something you would have never known in my care, and since I want for you so much more than I have obtained for myself, I gave you to my dear friends Caroline and Ethan to raise, to teach and to love. They will cherish you and demonstrate what love between a husband and wife is meant to be.

Rebecca's Reveries

I hope as you read this that you have found someone who adores you as dearly as Ethan adores Caroline and whom you cherish as much as Caroline cherishes Ethan.

Rebecca paused and looked up at Mitch who lifted his hand from where it rested behind her on the back porch and put his arm around her shoulder. He leaned over to kiss her cheek, and then she continued to read.

I loved your father in such a way, but I made mistakes that I shall always regret. But of all the things I regret, I never regretted being your mother, if only for a small season.

Forgive me, little one, for not being able to give you more. I pray that one day you will understand and that we may meet again. Jemima and your parents will always know where I am should you ever need me.

With all my love,

Your mother, Sabrina Mapleton

"Mitch! Grandma knows where she is!" Rebecca gasped and brushed the tears from her eyes. She quickly reached over and began placing the items back into the hatbox. "Here, help me put these things away so we can go talk to Grandma!" Mitch assisted Rebecca in replacing all of the contents of the box save the letter addressed to Rebecca. Then she grasped Mitch's hand, handed him the hatbox and started toward the

189

front door. Jefferson walked by just as the couple entered the house.

"Jefferson, where's Grandma?" Rebecca asked still clutching Mitch's hand as her right hand held her letter.

"She's sewin' in the livin' room, Miss," Jefferson nodded.

Mitch and Rebecca entered the living room to find Jemima sitting in her rocker by the fireplace working on a new cross stitch.

"Grandma, I found this letter addressed to me from Sabrina! She says you know where she is. Please tell me where she is!" Rebecca rushed to kneel at Jemima's knees, searching the elderly woman's deep brown eyes.

Jemima smiled and her eyes twinkled, "She's married now and lives in Chattanooga."

"You're kiddin?" Mitch's eyes widened and glanced down at Rebecca.

"You mean she's been this close all this time and I never knew?" Rebecca asked incredulously.

Jemima shrugged her shoulders, "Ain't that the way it always is? The best things in life are always directly under our noses." Jemima chuckled.

"Well, I want to meet her!" Rebecca exclaimed and rose to her feet.

"Bert and Edmund have taken off with the carriage and will be gone most o' the day. But we could go in the mornin' if you like," Jemima smiled.

"Oh, I don't want to wait until mornin'!" Rebecca whined.

"You've waited nearly eighteen years, what's another night?" Jemima chuckled at Rebecca's impatience. "It'll give you some time to sleep on what you'll say to her anyway."

"Oh, I hadn't thought of that! What *will* I say to her?" Rebecca nervously turned to Mitch.

"Just be yourself, Becca and let her talk. She's the one that'll have things to say, I'd imagine," Mitch suggested.

Rebecca put her hands to Mitch's chest, "Oh I'm so excited! You will come with us won't you?"

"You sure you want me to?" he hesitated.

"Well, of course, silly! I never would've figured all this out without you!" She reached up and touched his cheek tenderly and he grabbed her arm with his hand and kissed her wrist. Jemima noted their affectionate exchanged in wide-eyed wonder.

Rebecca turned to see her Grandmother's expression and began to explain, "Grandma, in all the excitement, I almost forgot!"

"What's that?" Jemima asked.

"Mitch and I are going to be married," Rebecca smiled at Jemima and then turned to gaze lovingly into Mitch's twinkling gray-blue eyes.

Jemima jumped to her feet letting her sewing drop to the floor and put her arms around the couple, "I just knew it! I just knew it! I'm so happy for you two!"

"Thank you, Ma'am" Mitch smiled.

"So when's the big day?"

"We," Rebecca hesitated and looked at Mitch who finished for her.

"We haven't decided on a date yet."

191

"Do you think Sabrina would come for the wedding?" Rebecca asked Jemima.

"Why of course, I'm sure she wouldn't miss it for the world! She knows you're here, ya know."

"She does?"

"I visited her before you arrived and told her you were comin'. I also sent her a post the other day and told her about your dreams."

"What did she say about that?"

"I haven't heard back from her yet," Jemima shrugged her shoulders.

"Oh, I hope it doesn't make her nervous that I know all of that," Rebecca winced.

Jemima patted Rebecca's back, "Don't worry yourself about that. Sabrina will be relieved that you understand her now."

Rebecca saddled Midnight and led him out of the stable as the sun set in a brilliant display of pinks, purples and violet streaming clouds. Mitch was breaking in one of the new horses Edmund bought at the last auction as Rebecca passed him, waved and Midnight took off at a gallop up the hill. Rebecca paused at the crest to enjoy the sunset and thought about how blessed she was to finally know the truth and to be meeting Sabrina the next day. After all the haunting memories, it all still didn't seem real, but tomorrow everything would become tangible.

Rebecca's Reveries

Rebecca nudged Midnight's sides, setting an easy gait toward the meadow. The field had been immaculately trimmed and bails of hay scattered here and yon. As she approached the knoll, an eerie fog rolled from the battlefield, across the creek and started toward her. Rebecca's heart raced as if the rolling fog were alive and chasing her. She turned Midnight and started back toward the hill. Hearing the distinct tromping of another set of hoof beats, she looked back over her shoulder to find a caped rider rushing toward her, the fog thick and billowing on his horse's heels. Rebecca kicked Midnight's sides, her heart beating violently as fear gripped her. Again she peered over her shoulder to see the long flowing hair and green luminous eyes of the caped rider.

"Green eyes!" she gasped as the rider gained on her position. The next thing Rebecca knew, she was being torn from her horse onto the apparition's stead. She looked up into the dark cape, screamed and fainted in utter fright. Midnight continued up the hillside, bolting riderless down the wooded embankment, finally slowing at the stables where he stopped just outside the door.

Seeing Midnight returning without Rebecca, Mitch's blood coursed through his veins, throbbing at his temples as he jumped off the horse he was training and ran toward the stable. Jumping over the fence he reached the stallion, "Midnight, where's Becca!" Quickly, Mitch climbed into the saddle, turned the horse and headed back for the hill. In a flash, Mitch reached the crest, only to find the fog rolling forward, engulfing the hickory trees and boulders.

"Where is she, boy?" Mitch muttered to the stallion. He loosened the reins hoping Midnight would lead him to

Rebecca. Midnight moved forward, and suddenly stopped, raring his head and neighing at the spot where Rebecca had been lifted from his back. Mitch peered around, but saw nothing. He leapt off the horse and knelt on the ground searching for clues.

"I can't see anythin' in this soup!" Mitch climbed atop the animal and headed back to the house. He jumped off the horse, and flew in the front door yelling at the top of his longs, "Jefferson! Bert! Mr. Marchant! Come quick!"

When no one came, Mitch started toward Edmund's study and knocked as he shoved open the door. "Sir, come quick! Rebecca's horse has returned without her and I can't see anythin' for the fog!"

Edmund stood, grabbed his coat and started toward the entry. "Jefferson! Come on!" he bellowed at the servant who had just entered the foyer. "Rebecca's missin'. Grab a lantern and come on!"

"Yes Sir!"

"Meet us at the hill!" Mitch instructed as he climbed atop Midnight, stopped at the stables and lit two lanterns. Edmund caught up with him and Mitch handed him a lighted lantern. Climbing atop their horses, Jefferson came running from behind carrying a lantern and entered the stable to find a horse.

Mitch and Edmund started up the now fog-covered hill. "Midnight stopped right here earlier. I'm thinkin' something must've happened to her here." Mitch held up his lantern peering around in the gray fog. Edmund turned as he heard Jefferson's horse ascending the hill and the glow of his lantern approached.

"All right, I'll take the left, Jefferson you go down the center and Mitch you take the right end o' the field and we'll comb it slowly and see if we can find her," Edmund instructed.

"Yes, Sir," Jefferson nodded and started down the center of the field as Mitch headed toward the right.

"Rebecca! You here?" Mitch called.

"Miss Rebecca, where are you?" Jefferson's voice echoed through the fog.

After an hour of searching, the three men met atop the hill, "Did you find anything?" Edmund asked Mitch.

"No, did you?" Mitch answered.

"Not a thing," Edmund muttered.

"Me neither," Jefferson shook his head.

"What on earth could've happened to her?" Mitch ran his hands through his thick blonde hair as a horrible panic seized him.

"Do you think…" Jefferson hesitated, not wanting to increase Mitch's obvious distress.

"What, Jefferson," Edmund prodded.

"Do you think she could've fallen into the creek?" Jefferson suggested.

"I hope not! It's freezin'!" Mitch gasped.

"Let's go back to the house and see if she's returned," Edmund recommended.

"We can't stop lookin' for her!" Mitch panicked.

"We're not stoppin'. Let's just look for her at the house. If she's not there, I recommend we start the search again in the mornin'." Edmund instructed.

"She can't stay out here all night!" Mitch held up his lantern, peering around some more, hoping that somehow Rebecca would emerge from the fog.

"Let's look back at the house and if you want to keep lookin' out here after that, then you're welcome to, but it's a waste o' time until this fog lifts," Edmund muttered.

Mitch nudged his horse and took off toward the house. He quickly tied Midnight's reins around a front porch column and ran up the steps jumping two at a time. He didn't bother to knock, but flung open the door and began calling her name, "Rebecca! Becca! Are you here?"

Jemima hurried down the stairs, "Mitch, what's goin' on? What're you yellin' about?"

"Rebecca! Have you seen her?"

"No, why?"

"She's missin'!"

"What?"

"I saw her go up over the hill and then only a little while later Midnight returned without her. Edmund, Jefferson and I've combed the back part o' the property, but in all this fog, we can't see much and we can't find her. We were hopin' she came back to the house,"

"Oh my!" Jemima flung her hand to her heart. "I'll help you look!" Jemima flung open every door upstairs and searched each room thoroughly while Mitch hunted downstairs. Shortly, Edmund, Jefferson, Bert and Hilda joined them in the search. They scoured the entire house, the yard, the stables, and the barn, but she was nowhere to be found. Finally Mitch informed the others that he would return to the hill, light a fire and stay the night there in hopes that she would see the light and find her way back through the fog.

Mitch built a fire in a clearing on the hill and walked around the property one more time, calling out to her, but he still heard no reply. Finally, he bundled up next to the roaring fire, hoping that she would return.

When morning broke, the fog had cleared and Mitch made one more search around the property and all along the creek, but he found nothing. He put out the fire and headed back to the house. Entering the front door, Jefferson greeted him, "Any luck?"

"No, I take it she didn't return?"

"No, we haven't seen her."

"How could she just disappear like this?" Mitch ran both hands through his thick rumpled hair.

Edmund headed for the front door, "Get some breakfast, Mitch. I'm goin' into town to round up some men to help us search for her. Jefferson, make sure he eats somethin'. He's gonna need his energy."

"Yes, Sir," Jefferson nodded and took Mitch by the arm and pointed him in the direction of the dining room.

Rebecca lay in a dank cave, covered with a blanket and her hands tied behind her back. In her unconscious condition, visions of the past took possession of her mind.

"Sabrina, I hope you'll consider my offer," he took both her hands in his.

"It's very thoughtful of you. It really is, but I just can't accept," her heart felt pity for the man in front of her.

"But you could keep the baby this way. If we were married, I could take care of you both. I would love the baby as if it were my own, Sabrina. I promise you that."

"I know you would. But, I want the baby to grow up in a home with a father and mother who love each other so that the child will always feel secure and happy," she explained.

"I love you, Sabrina. You know I always have," he leaned over and kissed her hand.

"And I love you, dear Edmund, but not that way. You're like my brother," she put her hand softly to his cheek.

"It's cause o' the way I treated Grant isn't it? I'm sorry about that. I shouldn't 've been so hard on you both," his head cast down and he stared at his feet.

"No, that's not it at all. You were right to be hard on us. We were wrong to do what we did. I just can't marry you. It wouldn't be fair to you or to the baby," she explained.

"And it's fair for the baby to never know its mother? Think about what I'm offerin' ya, Sabrina! I'm offerin' you a father to your child, a roof over your head, everythin' you and the child will ever need and a husband who's devoted to you and loves you."

"I'm sorry Edmund. I've already made my decision. Ethan and Caroline will take the baby and love it as their own. They want a baby so badly and it seems like the right thing to do. It would be selfish of me to deny the baby the opportunity to be raised by two parents who love each other that much."

"You could learn to love me, Sabrina," Edmund made one last plea.

"I've made my decision, Edmund. Please don't ask me again," she rose from her seat and left his study.

When Rebecca awoke, a fire burned in the center of the cave knocking the chill out of the otherwise cool, dank cavern and providing warmth in contrast to the cold dirt floor upon which she sat. Struggling and twisting she attempted to free herself of her bonds, but both her hands and feet were tied securely. Remembering the horror of her green eyed captor she hesitated to scream for help and she closed her eyes against the possibility of the returning apparition.

The hours of the night drug on endlessly for Rebecca for she couldn't get comfortable enough to sleep. Amidst the terrified anticipatory thoughts of the apparition's return, she spent the hours feeling compassion for her poor Uncle Edmund whose only love had rejected him and for her mother who lost both her child and the man she loved. Imagining that she lay securely within Mitch's strong arms, she finally succumbed to exhaustion and drifted off to sleep in the early hours of the morning.

Twenty men gathered at Soquili, some with hunting dogs, some with guns and rifles. Edmund organized them all into parties and Jemima brought Rebecca's scarf for the dogs to catch her scent. Just as Edmund was about to send out the parties, Dave and Stephen Phillips rode up on their horses.

"We hear you need help searchin' for your niece," Dave called to Edmund. Mitch stiffened as he saw Stephen.

"Yes, she's been missin' since last night. What are you two still doin' here?" Edmund asked.

"We've been in town on business and heard about Miss Rebecca over at the General Store. We'd like to help you search," Dave offered. "Stephen's just been beside himself with worry ever since he heard and insisted that we come help with the search."

"We do appreciate this! We can use all the help we can get," Edmund shook Dave and Stephen's hands.

Something about Dave and Stephen Phillips' appearance made Mitch nervous, but he shook it off realizing that most likely his nerves were on edge because he'd had very little sleep the night before and he had to admit that he would feel a disliking for anyone who showed an expressive interest in Rebecca.

The morning rapidly became afternoon and as Mitch searched an area inside the battlefield along the creek, he heard rustling leaves ahead of him. Quietly he crept forward and hid behind a tree. In front of him Stephen knelt by a large stump, pulled a pocket knife from a hole in the stump and threw leaves on top of the cavity. Mitch waited for him to rise and continue on and stepped lightly toward the stump. The aroma of moss and rotting leaves filled his senses as he reached his hand in, brushing aside the damp dew covered leaves, to reveal the cavity within the stump.

To his surprise, he found a black carpet bag and pulled it from the large stump. Opening it to look inside, his mouth dropped open and he reached in to retrieve a marble-handled pistol. He traced his fingers over the gold engraved initials of SRP on the handle. Mitch carried the bag in one hand and shoved the pistol in his pocket as he followed Stephen at a distance.

After traveling through the forest for about five minutes, Stephen looked around in various directions and crept into the mouth of a rocky cave. Mitch waited for him to enter and then quietly followed him, the musty cool air hitting his face as he stepped inside. Stephen lit a lantern and wound his way through the corridors unaware of Mitch who maintained a safe distance but pursued close enough to see the lantern light moving ahead of him.

"Stephen!" Mitch could hear Rebecca's voice cry out and he quickly hid in a crevice watching as Stephen ran to Rebecca's side and knelt in front of her.

"Oh Rebecca! I've been so worried about you!" he pulled his pocket knife from his back pocket and cut the ropes which bound her feet and hands. He kissed the red marks that the ropes had made on her wrists then placing his hands on either side of her face, he showered kisses on her cheeks, "I'm so relieved that I've found you! I've been so worried about you!"

"Thank you! Thank you for finding me!" She rose abruptly as his kisses moved to her lips. Stephen stood in front of her and put his hands on either side of her face, "How in the world did you get out here?"

"Something carried me here!"

"Something?" What do you mean?"

"It sounds crazy, but I believe it was Old Green Eyes! It pulled me from my horse and I saw the luminous green eyes and the long flowing hair on a caped apparition just before I fainted with fear. The next thing I knew I woke up in this cave, but the ghost was gone!"

Stephen put his arms around her holding her close and stroking her hair, "It's all right now. I won't let anything hurt you ever again."

"There never was anybody gonna hurt her but you, Phillips," Mitch stepped from the crevice and pointed the pistol at Stephen's back.

"Mitch? What are you doin' with that gun?" Rebecca gasped.

"Protectin' you from your green-eyed monster!" Mitch exclaimed and reached into the bag with his free hand and pulled out a wig.

"What?" Rebecca looked to Stephen, "What's goin' on?"

"Looks like Mitch here is Old Green Eyes and he's come to finish the job!" Stephen accused.

"Bull! You're the one who's done this! Rebecca, I saw Phillips pullin' his pocketknife from an old stump outside. When I went to see what he was up to, I found this bag with this wig, a cape and his green eyed monster mask inside it. This pistol with his initials on it was also in the bag. Look at it – SRP – Stephen R. Phillips engraved on the handle!"

"Why? Why would you do this Stephen?" her eyes pleaded as he took her shoulders in his hands.

"I tell you it's not me. Garrison is settin' me up!"

"Why would Mitch need to set you up?" she asked.

"He wants you for himself. He's tryin' to make you love him instead of me," Stephen accused.

"That doesn't make any sense, Stephen. Mitch knows I love him. We're getting married. It's you that's done this, isn't it? You thought…" she stopped as his clutch grew tighter on her shoulders.

Mitch stepped closer to Stephen with the pistol pointed at his back, "You thought that if you scared Rebecca half out of her mind and then came to her rescue that she'd see you as her hero and marry you."

Stephen quickly spun Rebecca around so that she stood between Mitch and himself and he held the blade of his knife to her throat. "One step closer and I'll slit her throat, Garrison!"

"You coward! Put the knife down, Phillips!" Mitch demanded.

"You put the gun down first," Stephen demanded.

"Let her go," Mitch cocked the weapon and Stephen pressed the knife into Rebecca's flesh at the base of her neck. Rebecca screamed as the searing pain of the knife dug into her skin and the blood dripped down onto her dress.

"Don't think I won't kill her, Garrison! I'd just as soon see her dead as touched by the likes o' you!" Stephen's angry eyes flashed a crazed stare.

"All right, all right! Leave her alone. I'm puttin' it down!" Mitch disarmed the pistol and set it on the ground at his feet.

"Kick it over here," Stephen demanded.

Mitch kicked the pistol with his boot so that it sailed past Stephen and hit the cave wall behind him.

"Bend down, Rebecca" Stephen demanded as he pulled her to the ground and he squatted to reach the pistol. As he did so, his hand that held the knife moved slightly giving Rebecca a small opportunity to make a break for freedom. She quickly stomped Stephen's foot with her shoe and as he winced in pain, Mitch lunged forward, shoved Rebecca aside and tackled Stephen. Both men tussled for the pistol and in the process, Stephen's knife cut deep into Mitch's shoulder blade.

Rebecca rose to her feet screaming Mitch's name in panic as a shot rent the air and the two men lay in a heap on the cave floor. Rebecca held her breath as a man rose to his feet and stepped from the shadows.

"Oh Mitch!" Rebecca ran to him, throwing her arms around his waist and her lips met his in a feverish exchange. "You're bleeding!" she exclaimed as she looked to see his blood mingled with her own on her dress. Quickly she pulled her apron off and held it to his profusely bleeding wound. Mitch put his hand over it applying pressure to the injury.

"Are you all right?" he caressed her cheek with his free hand.

"I'm fine! You're the one who's wounded! Let's get you home," she took one look back in Stephen's direction to make sure he still lay unconscious.

"You're bleedin' too, Becca," Mitch pointed to the blood seeping from her clavicle.

"Oh, it's not bad," she pulled a handkerchief from her pocket and held it to her neck.

"Let's get the bag as proof," Rebecca quickly stuffed the wig back into the bag and Mitch picked it up and threw it over his unwounded shoulder.

"To think he'd go to such great lengths!" Rebecca marveled.

Mitch pulled her into his embrace and kissed her hair. "It's all right. It's all over now," he comforted.

As Rebecca and Mitch emerged from the cave, Jefferson and Edmund met them outside. "We heard a shot fire," Edmund dismounted his horse and stepped toward Rebecca. "Are you both all right?"

"Mitch has been wounded. You'll find Stephen Phillips inside, but I'm not sure if he's alive or dead, so be careful," she warned.

"What? Stephen Phillips has been wounded?" Edmund asked.

"He abducted Rebecca last night pretending to be Old Green Eyes," Mitch handed the bag to Edmund. "I saw 'im rummagin' through this bag and inside was this pistol with his initials on it." Mitch handed the pistol to Edmund.

"Why would Stephen do somethin' like this?" Edmund shook his head.

"I guess he thought if he scared Rebecca enough and then came to her rescue that she'd feel somethin' for him and marry him."

"Oh, Rebecca, I'm so sorry that I didn't see this comin'. I thought he realized how fruitless it was to try to win your affections away from Mitch, but I guess he was only foolin' me all along," Edmund's sorrowful expression made pity rise within Rebecca's heart. Her poor uncle, his heart broken all these years, living his life alone and now he was making himself feel guilty because he couldn't make another man understand the futility of mourning over an unrequited love.

Rebecca embraced her uncle and kissed his cheek. "It's all right, Uncle Edmund. You did all you could. Who would think he would act in such a way?" Edmund stood there dumbfounded by Rebecca's affections. Noting his expression Rebecca whispered in his ear, "I'm sorry Uncle. I've misjudged you and I was wrong." Edmund looked into her eyes, puzzled by her words and then gave her a quick embrace.

Edmund and Jefferson entered the cave and Mitch escorted Rebecca back to his horse which he'd tied to a tree. Mitch mounted the horse and helped Rebecca to climb up behind him. She wrapped her arms about his waist and leaned against his back to keep warm.

After a short while, Edmund and Jefferson caught up with them. Stephen's body lay draped across Edmund's horse. "He's dead," Edmund muttered as he passed them. "Don't know how I'm gonna tell his Pa. You two go on home. We're goin' for the sheriff."

Jemima greeted them when they arrived at Soquili. "My heavens! What's happened?" Jemima cried out seeing Mitch and Rebecca covered in blood as they stepped down from the horse. "Hilda, please go get Dr. Thurman!"

Mitch had become weakened from blood loss, so Rebecca put her arm around his waist and he leaned on her shoulder to climb up the front porch steps and through the front door.

"Do you think you can make it up the staircase, Mitch?" Jemima asked as she put a concerned hand to his forehead to see if he was warm.

"I think so," he muttered. Jemima and Rebecca supported him on either side and helped him up the steps to the spare bedroom.

"Harrison Thurman's a doctor. He's on the property helpin' with the search. Hilda will bring him shortly," Jemima explained as she and Rebecca helped Mitch lie down on the bed in the guest room.

Rebecca explained the events to Jemima while they waited and soon they heard Harrison Thurman's footsteps coming up the stairs.

"We're in here, Dr. Thurman," Rebecca called and the doctor appeared at the door with his medical bag.

"Rebecca's injured. Help her first," Mitch panted.

"Nonsense. I've just a scratch. Help him and then tend to me," Rebecca insisted.

The doctor turned to Rebecca, "What's all this blood from?"

"It's Mitch's. I've just got this small cut on my collar bone. But Mitch was stabbed and it looks deep. Please see to him first."

"All right," Dr. Thurman turned to Mitch and began tending to his wound.

"How handy that you're a doctor!" Rebecca exuded gratefully and winked at her grandmother.

Within a short time Dr. Thurman had bandaged Rebecca and dressed Mitch's shoulder wound, placing his right arm in a sling. "You'll need to be careful with that for a week or so. No heavy lifting or exertion until it's mended."

"And no horse breakin' until it's healed! Right doctor?" Rebecca interjected.

"Oh, you break horses?" Dr. Thurman asked.

"Yes, Sir. It's my job here," Mitch answered.

"Mrs. Marchant, see that he has a week to recuperate before he goes back to work," Dr. Thurman instructed.

"I can't lay off work for a whole week! Who'll teach my students and take care o' the horses?"

"I could help out," Rebecca volunteered.

"Yes, Rebecca could handle the most pressing matters, Mitch. You need to rest," Jemima agreed.

"See there, I knew you were after my job the first day I saw you run those steeples!" Mitch laughed, winked and then held his wound for the laughing caused his shoulder to ache.

"Come with us, Uncle Edmund!" Rebecca tugged Edmund's hand in an effort to pull him off the front porch toward the waiting carriage. Jemima already sat inside and Bert sat atop, ready to leave.

"Yes, Mr. Marchant, I'm sure she'd like to see you, Sir," Mitch encouraged.

"No, there's been too much water under that bridge and I think it's best if I just stay here," he shook his bald head adamantly.

"Edmund, stop bein' a stubborn ol' mule and just get in the carriage! You need to close this book and get on with your life," Jemima called out the window of the conveyance.

"It'll be good for you, Uncle, to make your peace with her," Rebecca tugged his hand. This time he budged slightly and Rebecca held his hand leading him toward the carriage.

Mitch ran ahead and opened the door for Edmund and Rebecca to climb in and then he took his place at Rebecca's side. He grabbed Rebecca's hand in his and smiled as the carriage moved forward and jostled down the dirt driveway and out to the main road.

It took nearly half an hour to reach Sabrina's house. Rebecca peered out the carriage window and smiled at the neatly manicured lawn and bright yellow two-story house with black shutters. "I like her house," Rebecca remarked to the others.

"Sabrina and Randall are hard workers. They have a nice little farm and take care of what they have," Jemima remarked as she too peered out the window toward the house. Bert parked the carriage out front and Mitch hopped out first and assisted the ladies from the carriage as Edmund took up the rear.

"I don't know about this," Edmund muttered under his breath as he reluctantly stepped out of the carriage. Rebecca backed up and slid her arm through Edmund's tugging him toward the house.

"Oh, come on, Uncle. She won't bite," Rebecca winked.

As the group stepped up onto the porch, the front door swung open and a twelve-year-old girl with jet black hair and brown eyes greeted them. "Can I help you folks?" she asked. Rebecca stared mesmerized by the young girl who looked so much like herself at that age. Surely this girl must be her little sister! A sister! Rebecca always wanted a little sister. Could it actually be true?

Jemima stepped forward, "Yes, dear. Is your mama here?"

"She's inside in the kitchen," the girl replied and a six-year-old boy came running from within the house. He too had the same jet black hair, except he had striking green eyes.

"Who is it, Katy?" he tugged his sister's skirt happily.

"Could you please tell your mama that her cousin Jemima and her family have come for a visit?"

"I'll do it!" the little boy exclaimed as he turned and ran back into the house.

Katy opened the door wider allowing them to enter. As the four stepped into the house, Edmund intentionally stood behind Mitch so that he wouldn't be readily noticed.

"Jemima!" Sabrina came from the kitchen wearing a blue dress, wiping her hands on her white apron. "It's so good to see you!" Sabrina embraced Jemima who stood in front of the others. "And who have you brought with you?" Sabrina looked to the others until her eyes fell on Rebecca. "Is it? It can't be!"

Rebecca shook her head affirmatively but when she opened her mouth to speak nothing came out.

"It sure is, this is Rebecca," Jemima put her hand on Rebecca's shoulder and nudged her toward Sabrina.

The pair stood examining one another. Sabrina looked so much like Rebecca with only a few wrinkles around the eyes and a bit of grey at her temples. Rebecca extended her hand and Sabrina took it and then they both relinquished the handshake and threw their arms around each other embracing for a long moment. When Rebecca released Sabrina, Sabrina's eyes welled with tears that spilt onto her cheeks. "I just can't believe you're here after all these years!"

"Who's here, Brina?" a large man wearing overalls and heavy work boots tromped in the back door. He wore a jacket over his red and blue flannel shirt and smoothed back his sandy brown hair as he peered at Rebecca with his emerald eyes.

Coming forward, he extended his hand to Rebecca, "You must be Rebecca!" His voice boomed and his eyes twinkled merrily.

"Yes, Sir," Rebecca curtsied slightly.

"This is my husband Randall, Rebecca," Sabrina introduced.

"So good to finally meet you Rebecca. I've heard so many wonderful things about you," Randall greeted, taking Rebecca's hand in a firm handshake.

"You have?" Rebecca wondered how they'd know enough about her to have heard wonderful things.

"Oh yes, Jemima's been kind enough to give us updates and well, dear Caroline wrote nearly once a month before she passed on," Sabrina brushed the tears from her cheeks. She grabbed Rebecca's hands, "Just look at you! You're beautiful – just like I knew you'd be!"

"Who've you brought with you here?" Randall extended his hand to Mitch who awkwardly shook Randall's hand with his left since his right was still in a sling.

"This is my fiancé, Mitch Garrison," Rebecca introduced.

"Fiancé?" Sabrina's brown eyes widened and Rebecca nodded excitedly. "Wait a minute, Mitch Garrison? You're the little stable boy from Soquili! I know you!" Mitch's dimpled grin widened from ear to ear exposing his bright white teeth. "My, my, how you've grown up into a handsome man, and captured my little Becca's heart!" Sabrina embraced him and kissed his cheek.

"And we brought Uncle Edmund along too," Rebecca turned and reached past Mitch to pull Edmund forward by his arm.

"How you doin' Mrs. Jacobs?" Edmund nodded.

"Goodness, Edmund, don't be so formal! Sabrina put her hands on Edmund's shoulders and looked back over her shoulder to her husband. "This is my sweet cousin Edmund, Randall." She pulled him to her and kissed his cheek. Rebecca believed Edmund's bald head turned a shade of pink.

"Good to see you again, Sabrina. You're as beautiful as always," he smiled.

"This is what you have to look forward to, Mitch," Randall put his arm around his wife and winked.

"Well, everyone sit down, sit down," Sabrina pointed to the sofa and chairs in the parlor. "Oh, and this is our daughter Katy and our son Gabriel." Sabrina a hand on each child's shoulder.

"Is this the girl in the picture?" Katy asked.

"Yes it is," Sabrina nodded. Katy ran from the room and Rebecca's eyebrows rose. She hoped she hadn't upset the girl in some way. Shortly Katy returned carrying a picture frame. She handed it to Rebecca, "See, my mama keeps your picture on her dresser in her bedroom. She told me and Gabe that someday our older sister would come to visit. We're so happy you've come!" Katy rushed forward and threw her arms around Rebecca's neck.

When Katy released her, Rebecca examined the photograph and then handed it to Mitch. "I had this taken on my sixteenth birthday."

"I like it," he smiled and held the photograph up to Sabrina.

"Caroline sent it to me," Sabrina took the picture and placed it on the mantel. "We have so much catchin' up to do!" Sabrina suddenly exclaimed. "Would you stay with us for a few days so we can visit?"

Rebecca looked to Mitch and then to Jemima, uncertain how to answer. "Well, I don't know. I didn't bring anything to wear."

"Oh we're the same size. You can wear some of my things and I'm sure Mitch won't be able to stand it too long without you so he can ride over and bring your own things tomorrow if you like. What do you say? Will you stay and get to know your brother and sister better?" The two children smiled expectantly up at her as they kneeled at her feet.

"All right, yes, I'd love to get to know you all better," Rebecca nodded and smiled at her new family.

"I'll go get the guest room ready!" Katy exclaimed and took off running up the stairs and Gabriel followed close behind.

"They're adorable," Rebecca smiled. "And to think, up until a few moments ago I didn't even know I had a brother and sister!"

The group stayed and chatted for a couple hours until Edmund rose and announced that he needed to get back to the farm to work and that Mitch needed to take care of the horses.

"Wait, I said I'd take care of the horses for Mitch!" Rebecca remembered.

"Oh, don't worry about it Rebecca. Jefferson and I'll handle it. You spend some time with your Mama. This is more important," Edmund patted Rebecca's shoulder.

"Thank you, Uncle," Rebecca stood up, hugged him and kissed his cheek. He still hadn't gotten used to her sudden affection for him. He'd spent so many years as a lonely old bear that the embrace of a pretty young girl – even if it was his niece – made him nervous. He almost blushed every time she kissed his cheek.

"It's all right, Mr. Marchant, she sets my heart to flutterin' every time she kisses me too," Mitch teased with a wink.

"Hmmpf," Edmund huffed and escaped from the house out to the carriage.

"We'll come get Rebecca on Saturday," Jemima hugged Sabrina goodbye and then kissed Rebecca's cheek. "You two have a grand time."

"We will," Rebecca smiled as she watched her grandmother leave the house. Mitch still waited inside for a moment to bid her farewell.

"Come on, Katy and Gabriel, let's give Rebecca a minute to say goodbye to her beau," Sabrina put her arms around each child's shoulder and they followed Randall upstairs.

Mitch put his left arm around her waist and pulled her to him, "I'm gonna miss you somethin' terrible."

"I'll miss you too, but it's only four days. Absence makes the heart grow fonder," she winked.

"I don't know that my heart can grow any fonder," he kissed her lips tenderly. "Talk to Sabrina about a date for the weddin'. I don't think I can wait much longer." He pulled her to him, kissing her warmly until he heard giggles from upstairs. They looked up to see Gabriel and Katy leaning over the banister giggling.

"How about a week from Saturday?" Sabrina called from upstairs as her head popped over the banister and peered down at them.

"I thought ya'll were givin' us a minute alone?" Mitch grumbled light-heartedly.

"Your minute's up," Sabrina chuckled.

Mitch looked at Rebecca who shook her head in agreement. "Sounds great to us!" Mitch ran to the door, opened it and hollered out to Jemima who sat waiting in the carriage.

"How 'bout a weddin' for a week from Saturday? Will that work for you?"

"Sounds perfect, now get on out here. It's gettin' cold!" Jemima motioned for Mitch to hurry along.

Mitch ran back to Rebecca and put his arm around her again and kissed her quickly, "Week from Saturday it is! I love you!"

"Love you too."

She kissed him one last time and he headed for the door, waving goodbye as he exited, "I'll see ya Saturday!"

Rebecca stood at the door and waved as the carriage rode away. Then she climbed the stairs to join the rest of her newfound family.

"This'll be your room while you're here," Sabrina pointed into a lovely guest room in which Randall had already lit a glowing fire to keep her warm.

"Gabe, Katy, let's go outside and take care of the animals and leave your Mama and Rebecca to catch up." Randall put a hand on each child's shoulder.

"Oh, can't we stay? I want to listen too!" Katy whined.

"Go ahead and run along now, you can have some time with Becca later," Sabrina answered.

Rebecca took Katy's hands, "We'll take a long walk together tomorrow – just the two of us and you can show me the farm and we'll get to know each other." Rebecca's solution seemed to satisfy the girl. She grinned and followed her father out of the room and Randall shut the door behind them.

Rebecca and Sabrina sat down and talked for hours. Rebecca told her about her life with Caroline and Ethan. Rebecca was surprised by how much Sabrina already knew about her. Sabrina left the room for a moment and returned with a bundle of letters that she had received from Caroline giving details on almost every month of Rebecca's life up until the time Caroline died.

Rebecca told her about coming to Soquili and meeting Mitch. She related her dreams and visions which had given her such incredible insight into Sabrina's life. She told her mother about looking through the hatbox and reading the letter she'd written her years before.

Sabrina pled with her, "I hope you can find it in your heart to forgive me for giving you up. Is there any way you can forgive me for that?"

"There's nothing to forgive. You were right. I needed to be raised by two people who loved each other like Ethan and Caroline did. The example of their love helped me avoid making a terrible mistake. I might've married Stephen had I not known what a happy marriage was like." Rebecca related the turmoil of earlier in the week when she had been abducted by Stephen Phillips and how Mitch had rescued her.

Sabrina embraced her in relief that not only had Rebecca been kept safe from harm, but also that she had forgiven her for her choice so many years ago. Sabrina told Rebecca about how she'd met Randall after leaving Soquili and moving to Nashville and how they had moved back to Chattanooga, bought the farm and began raising a family. Life had been good for Sabrina. She felt God had forgiven her somehow and given her a second chance.

Over the next few days, Rebecca came to love her mother, Randall and her little brother and sister. They welcomed her as if she had always been there. She wished she could take them home to Kentucky with her, but they promised to visit and she and Mitch would return to Georgia as often as they could.

Saturday soon arrived and Bert pulled up in the carriage outside. Rebecca peeked out the window and ran outside when Mitch stepped out of the carriage. His arm was out of the sling and he threw his arms around her, lifting her up into the air.

"Put me down Mitch, you'll hurt your shoulder!" she warned.

"Oh, I'm all right," he kissed her and she led him by the hand into the house where they spent a few remaining moments with Sabrina and her family.

"You'll be there for the weddin' – right?" Mitch asked as he and Rebecca started to leave.

"Of course we will! Wouldn't miss it for the world!" Sabrina hugged them both and they left her house. As she leaned on the doorframe watching them leave, Randall stood behind her, slipped his arms around her waist and kissed her long neck.

"You've been blessed, my love. Heaven's smilin' on ya," he whispered.

"Yes, indeed it is and I have no idea why," she brushed a tear from her cheek.

"You made a great sacrifice all those years ago, and this is God's way of showin' ya that not only are you forgiven for the past, but also that He loves you dearly."

Sabrina rubbed her husband's arm at her waist, laced her hands through his fingers and kissed his hand.

Epilogue

*R*andolph led Sabrina to the front of the little country church and sat down next to her in the pew. Mitch stood at the front of the chapel waiting nervously for his bride while Dr. Thurman escorted Jemima forward and she slid in next to Sabrina. Jemima squeezed Sabrina's hand and smiled as the music started.

"So when are we gonna do this?" Harrison Thurman whispered in Jemima's ear as he slid his arm around her shoulder.

Jemima's eyes widened as she looked up into his twinkling green eyes, "Anytime you're ready."

"I'm ready," he winked. "How 'bout next week?"

Jemima nodded her head affirmatively and Harrison leaned over to affectionately kiss her cheek.

As the organist played, Katy, Millicent and Emily walked down the aisle and took their places as Rebecca's bridesmaids and Gabriel carried the ring on a pillow.

Aunt Miriam peeked over her shoulder toward Rebecca who stood next to Edmund. "Isn't she beautiful, Dan?"

"She sure is! Who'd o' thought our little Rebecca would finally get up the nerve to get married," Dan chuckled.

"I knew when the right man came along she'd fall hard," Miriam squeezed her husband's arm.

"You nervous?" Edmund extended his arm to Rebecca.

"A little," she took his arm and her uncle kissed her cheek.

"You look beautiful, Rebecca. You could be your mother, wearin' your hair like that in that weddin' gown Mother made ya."

Rebecca smiled, thinking how grateful she felt to have Sabrina and her family in her life as well as Edmund and Jemima. God had not left her alone. He'd given her a good man and a wonderful family, just when she thought she'd lost everything. A tear glistened in her eyes as she wished that her parents could be there to share the day.

"One thing's different 'tween you two though," Edmund added. "You saved yourself for your one true love. You learned from the errors of the past and spared yourself the trauma of Sabrina's life. I'm proud o' ya for that. You're a good young woman, and I know Ethan and Caroline are proud of you too. Somewhere they're smilin' down on ya from heaven."

"Oh, Uncle Edmund, you are a sweetheart!" Rebecca kissed his cheek and he led her down the isle toward the man of her dreams. As Mitch took her hand in his, Rebecca knew that together they would pass their legacy of love on to the little ones who would join their home. For Rebecca Marchant, God had indeed made miracles from mistakes, treasure from tragedy and hope from hopelessness.

Rebecca's Reveries

About the Author

Marnie L. Pehrson and her
family purchased 24 acres of the
former hundred-acre, Battlefield
Stables bordering the
Chickamauga Battlefield at an
auction in 1996. She and her
sister's families designed and
built houses next to each other on the historic landscape
which inspired *Rebecca's Reveries*.

Marnie and her husband Greg are the parents of six children.
She is the founder of multi-denominational SheLovesGod.com
which hosts the annual SheLovesGod Virtual Women's
Conference the 3rd week of October each year. Subscribe to her
free weekly Bible study lesson on the site. Marnie has served
in many capacities within her church in presidencies of the
women's and children's organizations, as a Sunday School
teacher and pianist. Recent service as family history consultant inspired her foray into historical fiction.

Marnie is also an internet developer and consultant who
helps talented professionals deliver their message to the
online world. You may visit her projects through
www.PWGroup.com.

**Marnie welcomes reader comments and may be
reached at webmaster@SheLovesGod.com
or by calling 706-866-2295**

Other Books by Marnie Pehrson

Lord, Are You Sure?
ISBN 0-9729750-0-4, 152 pages
A roadmap for understanding how Heavenly Father works in your life, helping you understand why certain problems keep repeating themselves, how to break the cycle and unlock the mystery of why you encounter challenges and roadblocks on roads you felt inspired to travel.

10 Steps to Fulfilling Your Divine Destiny: A Christian Woman's Guide to Learning & Living God's Plan for Her
ISBN 0-9676162-1-2, 124 pages
Have you ever said to yourself, "I'd love to do great things with my life, but I'm just too busy, too untalented, too ordinary, too afraid, too anything but extraordinary"? Inside this book you'll learn how to reach your full God-given potential.

Journal/Workbook Companion for 10 Steps to Fulfilling Your Divine Destiny: A Christian Woman's Guide to Learning & Living God's Plan for Her
ISBN 0-9676162-2-0, 220 pages

Packets of Sunlight for Parents
Compiled by: Marnie L. Pehrson
144 pages, paperback
ISBN 0-9676162-4-7
Brighten your day with inspiration for parents of tots to teens!

Packets of Sunlight for American Patriots
Compiled by: Marnie L. Pehrson
ISBN 0-9676162-3-9, 108 pages
Let the founding fathers, reignite your love for
freedom!

A Closer Walk with Him
SheLovesGod Study Lessons Volume 1
by Marnie L. Pehrson
212 pages, paperback, ISBN 0-9729750-3-9
A collection of insights and ponderings on the scrip-
tures and how we can apply them to our everyday
lives. Great for the faith-lift you need in the morning,
just before bed, or whenever you need a quick boost of
inspiration. Each lesson is self-contained and
independent. Read them in any order the Spirit moves
you or read the 52 lessons in order as a yearly study
guide - it's up to you.

The Patriot Wore Petticoats
Historical Fiction, Scheduled for Release in 2004
by Marnie L. Pehrson
Daring "Dicey" Langston, the bold and reckless rider
and expert shot, saves her family and an entire
village during the American Revolution. Having faced
British soldiers, rushing swollen rivers, the "Bloody
Scouts," and the barrel of a loaded pistol, nothing had
quite prepared this valiant heroine for the heart-
pounding exhilaration she'd find in the arms of one
brave Patriot. Based on a true story about the author's
fourth great-grandmother. Learn more at
www.DiceyLangston.com

To order call 800-524-2307 or visit
www.SheLovesGod.com/bookstore